The Law of Falling Bodies

Jill Ciment

Poseidon Press

New York   London   Toronto

Sydney   Tokyo   Singapore

POSEIDON PRESS

Simon & Schuster Building
Rockefeller Center
1230 Avenue of the Americas
New York, New York 10020

POSEIDON PRESS is a registered trademark
of Simon & Schuster Inc.

POSEIDON PRESS colophon is a trademark
of Simon & Schuster Inc.

Designed by Chris Welch
Manufactured in the United States of America

10 9 8 7 6 5 4 3 2 1

Library of Congress Cataloging-in-Publication Data
Ciment, Jill, date
    The law of falling bodies / Jill Ciment.
        p.   cm.
    I. Title.
PR9199.3.C499L39   1993
813'.54—dc20   92–27120
                                              CIP

ISBN: 0-671-79451-5

For Arnold,
and in memory of Catherine Low

I wish to thank David Leavitt and Arnold Mesches for their generous input and many readings. I would also like to thank Bernard Cooper, Lesley Karsten, and Ann Patty for all their help and support.

Part One

The Law of Falling Bodies

Chapter One

When I was small, I believed that the atmospheres girdling the earth included an extra sphere. There was the blue-black stratosphere, the airy and weather-beaten trophosphere, and just below table height where I lived, a sphere about which I told no one—the kindersphere. My version of physics, pieced together from my mother's idiosyncratic view of the world, fell apart when applied to my lessons at school. Arithmetic, according to my teachers, was not personally involved in my mother's financial problems, meteorology didn't reflect her variable moods. Without these explanations, however, the world became an indifferent place and besides, there was something secretly thrilling about believing that no matter how often my mother and I moved, the planet's axis was always located somewhere in our house.

We lived all alone in an aluminum trailer and at least once a year, until Arthur rolled into our existence, we'd hitch it to our blue convertible and move on, a whir of clouds and sun mirrored in its aerodynamic shape. Sometimes, barreling down the highway, it looked as if we towed a sliver of the sky with our dented bumper. We were constantly changing address because, according to my mother, everybody was after us—her mail order customers, the Food and Drug Administration, even the postmaster general (in those years, I pictured him as a successful mailman with epaulets).

My mother sold aphrodisiacs. Her secret formula was diluted in perfume and from its pungent smell—a hybrid of pine and floral aerosol—I assumed an aphrodisiac was a species of flower. I'd just recently learned to divide the world into plant, animal, mineral, and gas. According to my mother, her customers fell into three subdivisions my teachers hadn't mentioned, "the ugly, the lame, and the mad." She advertised her perfume in the weekly tabloid, on the back page, in tiny print.

The tabloid fascinated me. The photographs were like nothing in my primer books—a blurred snapshot of a radiator whose piping whistles played the lost symphonies of Beethoven, a woman's face with and without a mustache. HUMAN HAIR GROWS .00000001 MILES AN HOUR. LADIES, MIRACLE WAX IS THE ANSWER! Most of the articles were incomprehensible to me and had to be read aloud by my mother. "When a loved one dies," my mother read, "don't give away their pets, don't throw out their houseplants! Scientists have discovered that the souls of those we've lost are held captive in inferior beings!"

At night, alone in my aluminum bedroom, discombobulated by our constant moving, I would get these images jumbled in my head until a houseplant was removing its thorns with wax and a human soul, imprisoned within the bars of a radiator, wept loudly and called me by my name.

I had no make-believe friends. My mother subscribed to the theory that by school age, my nature had already been woven with all the moral fiber she had available. I was on my own. The only fantasy I harbored was that the hours I spent being good—helping my mother read the road maps or enlarging my vocabulary with the tabloids—were tallied up by my former grade school teachers, whose moonlight jobs were to keep track of my life by radio transmitters implanted in me during a school nap. Compared with my mother's imagination, however, my own seemed elementary.

She said we were going to be millionaires. She said the past was the past. Whenever we pulled into a new trailer park, she'd immediately begin to rebuild our lives, hacking off a bad year there, adding in a good month here, until my memories hung from the miraculous rafters of her construction. At ten, I thought my mother possessed the basic principle of magnetism. If I got lost amid the unfamiliar trailers, all I needed to do was gravitate toward the nearest commotion—an argument about the rent, a fight over a parking spot: my mother was always in the center. At night, when we'd gaze up at the stars, after reading about flying saucers in the tabloid, she'd see every strange formation of lights in the sky as a possible visitation. Often, when I came home from school, she'd be transfixed at the window staring into outer space.

"What did you do in school today?"

I explained how we were given crayons and asked to draw where in the world we'd most want to live. I proudly held up my drawing of an anonymous metropolis.

"That's very good, Kim. But where are the windows? Where are the doors? I'm afraid it doesn't look like a skyline to me."

"What do you think it looks like, Mom?"

"A graph of my moods."

During the course of our travels, I attended twelve elementary schools and two junior highs. We lived in thirteen trailer parks. We drove over ninety thousand miles. I used to hope that when the numbers on our car's odometer reached zero again, our lives could begin anew. According to the tabloid, such things were possible: if it doesn't work out for you in this life, if your heart gives out, or your cells start exploding, you can have yourself flash-frozen and defrosted in a better world.

"Boy, I wouldn't mind having myself put in suspended animation until the postmaster general loses our trail," my mother said. "You're in the ninth grade, Kim—what's the statute of limitations?"

I thought she said the "*statue* of limitations" and I tried to imagine what it would look like. The only sculptures I'd seen were dinosaurs in dioramas. The only art I was familiar with were motel paintings of skys. And so, I envisioned a clay replica of my mother, larger than life, steering our blue convertible toward a gaudily painted and completely illusory sunset.

Only twice in those years did my image of my mother falter. The first time, we were rolling along a desolate highway when our tire blew. My mother killed the engine.

"I sure hope your radio transmitters are working tonight, kid. I sure hope your teachers are on the ball."

Then she leaned her forehead against the steering wheel.

I didn't say anything.

After a moment or two, to quell the unbearable stillness and roll us to safety, my mother turned over the ignition. The dashboard was revived into amber life. The wipers, rolling over the greasy windshield in languid arcs, turned the stars into brilliant prisms.

"I have no one," she said, "no one to watch over me."

You see, it was imperative that my mother continue to confuse the oily streaks on our dirty windshield with a sort of distant rainbow.

The second time, we were standing in line under the blue-washed ceiling of the Arcadia post office, gluing postage stamps on her perfume mail orders. My mother looked up at the cork bulletin board of wanted posters and remarked: "You know, any day now, we're probably going to see my picture up there. How do you think they'll describe me, Kim? Hair: brass. Eyes: red. Last seen going nowhere fast in a blue convertible."

I suddenly started to cry. An elderly farmer at the counter, and his Adam's-appled son, turned around and stared at us.

"Please . . . please don't cry, honey," my mother murmured, gently dabbing up my tears with her sleeve. "I was only joking."

I couldn't stop. You see, it had finally occurred to me that my mother was *unwanted* and if I didn't do something quick, the only cell she'd wind up in was the solitary confinement of her illusions.

About six months after that, late one night, we were caught in a horrendous electrical storm in the hills above Los Angeles. The road turned into a lightning-blue shiver and thunder caromed around the walls of the canyons. Whenever my mother drove during atmospheric disturbances, she experienced hallucinations. We swerved for an armless apparition—it turned out to be a dripping fire hydrant. She braked for a flying hoopskirted skeleton—it metamorphosed into an escaped umbrella. Then Arthur's black Packard rolled out of his driveway and into our lives. His car was not spectral. We were hit.

There are a couple of laws that tell what an object does when it is allowed to fall without anything stopping it. These are called the Laws of Falling Bodies. The first law says that, under the influence of gravity alone, all bodies alike, regardless of their weight or size, fall at the same velocity. The second law says that in a void without air, the density or shape of the body doesn't affect the fall either. Consequently, a one-hundred-and-thirty-pound woman and a ninety-five-pound fifteen-and-a-half-year-old girl will hit the ground at the same time if they've made their descent in a perfect vacuum.

My mother and I landed on wet grass, road maps flying around us like startled fowl. The convertible stood deep in shrubbery, its doors open, its black-and-white-wall tires spinning senselessly. Our trailer was banked on the curb, its aerodynamic rear end hideously squashed.

I sat up.

A few feet away, in a whirlwind of mud, chrome, rubber, and rain, Arthur's Packard came to a spinning stop, and he stumbled out, his tall, dazed, dark-haired figure staggering a bit before sinking down beside us on the sopping lawn. His chin was cut and he was shaking. For a couple of minutes no one spoke. The only sounds were an occasional pop of thunder and our car radios crackling over the drumming rain: his played a melodic symphony, ours hissed and squabbled with a call-in talk show: "Night owls, pick up your phones. The topic tonight is bomb shelters. Would you take your neighbor in?"

He rubbed his eyes, looked at me, blinked, then stared at my mother. "Are you two all right?" he asked nervously.

I nodded, but my mother didn't stir or say anything. Her mohair sweater was torn and one of her leather clogs was missing. Surrounded by blowing road maps, her bare white foot appeared to me to be the stillest, palest point on earth.

"Stay calm and don't let her move," he said. "I'll be right back." He wrenched his attention from her and pointed to a yellow porch light under a shivering eucalyptus. "I'm just going into my house to phone the police for help."

"Really," my mother said, "that won't be necessary."

She groped for my hand. She slowly sat up. In her bedazed state, she looked around, more stunned than frightened. Then she touched, with grass-stained fingers, the purplish protuberance swelling on her forehead.

Arthur peeled off his raincoat and covered my mother with its glistening folds. "What's your name?" he asked.

Her blue eyes stared vacantly up at him, then drifted toward me. For a moment her muddled gaze cleared. "Gloria," she said softly.

"Do you remember what happened, Gloria? Do you know where you are?"

Her eyes sank back into swampy confusion. She shook her head.

Arthur took a deep breath. "Gloria, can you tell me what day of the week it is? Who is our president?"

My mother perceived time as elastic; we didn't have a voting address.

"Ask me who the postmaster general is," she suggested.

Arthur turned his head very slowly and looked at me, his large blue-black eyes filled with wild anxiety. "I think we should take Gloria to the hospital," he said. Then, noticing the brush burns on my left knee, he asked, "Are you sure you're all right?" I said I was. We both crouched over my mother. "Gloria," he asked, "do you think you can walk to my car?"

My mother said she could walk but she didn't want to go to any hospital. She wanted to get our car out of the shrubbery. She said if she could just catch her breath and find her other shoe, she'd like to get back on the highway again and make Indio by dawn.

Her face looked bloodless.

Obviously my mother didn't grasp the full calamity of the accident, and I was so chilled, and numb, and wet, and frightened, all I wanted to do was go home.

I asked Arthur if he could help me get my mother out of the rain and into our trailer.

He stared at the mangled aluminum on the curb, at his yellow porch light, again at the trailer. What choice did he really have? With gentle coaxing and a firm grip, he hoisted us up onto our feet and, slinging my mother's limp arm around his neck, half led, half carried us over the slippery turf into his house.

There was a powder-blue vestibule and wine-colored living room with bamboo blinds, Hawaiian furniture, and a petrified-wood coffee table on which three bright red-and-blue *Life* magazines lay meticulously fanned. My mother and I slumped on the sofa. Arthur rushed into the kitchen and came back with an ice pack for my mother's lump.

Was she sure she wouldn't change her mind and go to the hospital?

She was positive.

He asked me to watch her while he made a quick phone call.

My mother looked up from under the frosty pack and wanted to know who he was calling.

A doctor friend of his, just to make sure he was handling this right.

It was exactly eight minutes past two by the brass numbers on a sunburst-shaped clock on the wall. I closed my eyes for a moment and rested my head on my mother's shoulder. Outside, something loud and metallic—a garbage can lid? one of our hubcaps?—clattered onto the asphalt.

Arthur returned with a first-aid kit and a hastily scribbled list and sat down beside us. "Gloria," he asked, "are you at all queasy? Nauseous in any way?"

My mother inclined her head to one side and thought for a moment. On the contrary; she believed she was hungry.

Arthur's whole face relaxed. Evidently this was a good sign. He fixed us warm tea and gave us two aspirins each. My mother and I were beginning to shiver from head to toe. He poured us thimblefuls of brandy from a decanter. My mother downed hers and licked the last drops out of her shot glass with the tip of her tongue. He brought us blankets and towels and helped us out of our sodden cardigans. He seemed to have a dozen hands: opening the first-aid kit, attending to the bruises on my left knee, peeking under the ice pack to see if my mother's lump had stabilized. He kept asking her if she was dizzy. His own gait was unsteady, his eyes red-rimmed, his disheveled black hair gemmed with raindrops. Suddenly he stopped, rubbed his eyes with his fists, took a deep breath, and sank onto the sofa beside us. For a couple of minutes he just sat there, his head in his hands. My mother and I looked at each other, then stared straight ahead: she at the blue bubbles suspended in the ice pack, me at the phantom automobiles visible through a foggy windowpane.

"I am so sorry," he said at last, "so deeply sorry."

He told us that he never saw our car coming. "It just loomed up. Out of nowhere. Huge. In my windshield. I tried to brake but it was all like a mad dream—the pedal, the horn, nothing was where it was supposed to be. If only I had—"

He bowed his head and composed himself. Was there anyone he should call tonight? A relative? Friends? Was someone expecting us?

My mother and I had no one but I didn't want him to think we weren't wanted somewhere, by someone, so I said that I would call Aunt—I glanced around the room for inspiration: Eddie Fisher was on the cover of *Life* magazine—Aunt Liz in the morning.

My mother's eyes shifted slightly to the left, peered curiously up at me, then closed.

He guessed in that case, probably the best thing to do right now would be to let my mother get some sleep. He guessed I probably wanted to rest too.

I said I was exhausted.

Without a word he slipped into his master bedroom; I could hear by the squeak of bedsprings and the snap of sheets that he was changing his linens. "Gloria," he said, helping my mother up the carpeted steps and easing her onto his king-size mattress, "please don't worry about anything tonight. I'll be right in the next room if you or Kim need me." He tucked her under a patchwork quilt. "We'll figure things

out in the morning. What to do about the cars, the doctor.
We can go over all the practical—"

My mother's whole frame shuddered with a yawn.

"It's not important now," Arthur said.

He slung an extra wool blanket over the wagon wheel
footboard and motioned me to follow him into the hall.

I apologized about the mess: my mother and I had both
left wet effigies of ourselves on his sofa cushions.

He said it didn't matter. He said as long as my mother
and I were okay, that was all that mattered.

His head was inclined against the doorjamb, his hands
idle at his sides. He wore sandy-brown trousers and black
wing tip shoes. He was in his mid-forties and very handsome
in a cigar-store Indian sort of way. "Listen," he said, "your
mother's probably just going to sleep through the night
but"—he lowered his voice—"if she wakes up or starts
acting strangely in any way, you should wake me immediately."

These were the signs I should look for: dizziness, swings
of mood, hallucinations.

"Do you think you'll be okay?"

I thought so.

I stepped back into the room and he quietly shut the door
behind me.

"Kim?" my mother called softly.

I sat down beside her.

"May I have a glass of water?"

I fetched her a glass of water; she gulped it down, fell
back on the pillows, and was instantly asleep.

I crawled under the quilt beside her.

Sometime before dawn, however, when I stirred from

sleep, I found her sitting up in bed, absolutely lost to this world. The rain had stopped and all was very still and quiet and dark, save for the stippled moonlight pouring in through the bamboo blinds.

She wanted to know where she was.

I told her.

She wanted to know what had happened and why she had a headache.

I explained.

She wanted to know when we were leaving.

At the crack of dawn, I lied.

Then I got her to lie down again and removed the ice pack (now only a tranquil blue pool in a glassy bag) and plumped up her pillow and straightened the quilt and fetched her another glass of water. I wanted to get her as comfortable as possible in this big bed, under these unfamiliar sheets, in this strange house because, in point of fact, we had absolutely nowhere else to go.

Chapter Two

Next morning, my mother didn't remember where she
was or what I had told her. When she opened her eyes,
she looked as if she were coming out of an ether dream. Her
face was pale, her focus glassy, and during the night, her
lump had turned blue black and had swollen to the size of
a child's fist.

I went to get Arthur. He'd spent the night in his den,
cramped in an armchair, his long legs up on a hassock, a
reading lamp burning beside him.

I padded across the carpet and gingerly shook him awake.

For a moment he, too, didn't seem to grasp where he was
or who was fetching him back into the daylight.

Then he was at our bedside, scrutinizing my mother's
lump, dialing his doctor friend. By the time his friend
arrived, my mother had conked out again, a pink hand
shielding her eyes from the noon light. The doctor, a
bulldog-jowled man in checkered slacks, took one look at
her dark contusion and opened his black bag.

My mother lifted her bruised head. She said she didn't want to be examined.

When the doctor finally got her to sit up, cupping the cold bell of his stethoscope under her left scapula, she said it wasn't necessary. When he asked her to look up and down, left and right, training the beam of his penlight into her glassy stare, she said she felt perfectly all right. She kept fidgeting while he checked her reflexes and evaded any questions about her medical history. But when he asked her to spread her arms and she couldn't touch the tip of her nose— no matter how hard she concentrated—with either of her bitten fingernails, I saw a look of blank terror cross her face.

With a gentle pat on the shoulder, the doctor explained to her that she had sustained a concussion and that unfortunately there was nothing he could really do for her other than to prescribe complete bed rest.

My mother let out a deep sigh. She wanted to know for how long.

The doctor shrugged. These things took time.

She wanted dates. She wanted him to be specific.

"Gloria," he said, sitting down beside her. Did she mind if he called her Gloria?

My mother said she didn't.

"I've got to be perfectly honest with you, Gloria. With this type of a concussion, complicated by a rather hefty contusion"—he palpated her bruised forehead again—"it's going to be at least two or three weeks. I'm sorry. I wish I had better news for you."

Next he asked me to sit down, running me through the same series of tests: I checked out fine. He patted me on the head and told me to take it easy for a day or two, to put some ice on my scraped knee if it hurt.

Then he folded up his black bag and, taking Arthur by the arm, led him behind closed den doors where he loudly admonished him for not having driven us directly to the hospital the night before, handed us over to professionals, and been done with—how should he put it?—this unfortunate but ludicrous situation. What the hell was Arthur planning on doing with us?

I turned to my mother but she had faded again, her pale arms outstretched on the quilt.

A moment later, Arthur appeared in the room asking me if I wanted to call my aunt now, or anyone else for that—

I said we had no one else.

He looked down at my groggy mother. I could use the phone in his den.

I perched on his walnut wood desk, my socked feet on the swivel chair. For a moment Arthur hung back in the shadows, not really eavesdropping but burning to listen and see if Aunt Liz would take us off his hands.

I picked up the receiver, enacting a conversation with a long-distance operator in—I glanced at his *Atlas: Alaska to Zululand*—Fairbanks (Arthur's face fell), waited a couple of seconds, simulated a warm hello, and assured the dial tone that Mom and I were okay.

Then I padded back to my mother, lay down on the quilt beside her, and put my hand on her cheek.

About twenty minutes later, Arthur came in carrying two dinner trays. He set them down on the maple night tables and pulled up a chair. He didn't say anything about our having to leave. He didn't say anything about our taking over his bed. He just sat with us going over the arrangements he'd made for repairing our trailer and car, while I silently consumed my soup and eggs (my mother was too weary to touch hers). And when she conked out again, her face buried in the crook of her arm, you could tell he wanted desperately to say something reassuring to me. He picked up her paper napkin from the floor; he started to speak but only shook his head.

The dinner trays had scenes of pioneer life enameled on their white tops—a log cabin, a hearth, an Indian, a prairie—and to fill the long silence in the fast-fading daylight, while I spooned the last of my soup, he and I talked about life on the plains. He pointed to the laminated hearth and said his great-grandfather had built one exactly like that. I pointed to the prairie and speculated on what it must have been like to be out there in the middle of nowhere surrounded by peril and dust.

That evening, as soon as my mother and I were alone again, I tried to talk to her and find out what was going to happen to us now. I asked her if she thought Arthur might let us stay for a while. I wanted to know where we'd go if he didn't.

The lights were off and only a pale arc of streetlamp penetrated the darkness. My mother lay curled on her side (my cheek was on the pillow beside her) and whenever she'd start to close her eyes, gently, so as not to hurt her, I'd nudge her shoulder, and tug on her sleeve, and try to beckon her back out of her torpor. I needed her to talk to me.

Once she tried to sit up and take me around and comfort me, leaning on my shoulder, but I could see, even in this dim light, that she was many miles away.

I lowered her head back onto the pillows. I let her drift off. Then I just sat there for what seemed like hours, stunned by my solitude, staring at my bruised knee (two red welts were forming a lilac isthmus between them). Around

two I couldn't bear to sit there any longer. I slipped on my
pedal pushers and wandered into the hall, taking a seat on
the carpeted steps. I must have made some sort of noise
because a moment later Arthur appeared at the top of the
staircase, knotting up his Scotch plaid robe.

"I couldn't sleep," I quickly explained.

"Neither could I," he said.

But you could see he'd just woken up: his hair was rum-
pled and when he came down the steps, he walked with the
baffled gait of one who thinks he's still treading the rubbery
floor of sleep.

He sat down a couple of steps above me and together we
stared into the dark living room. An airplane droned overhead and somewhere down the block I could make out the
thunderclap of a tin garbage lid closing, followed by the
clink of chain that manacled it to its can.

Arthur pretended to look out the window but I saw him
try to wake himself up by rubbing his eyes with the heels
of his hands.

"Kim, are you hungry?" he asked.

"Not really."

"Some tea?"

I said I guessed that sounded okay and I followed him
into the yellow-walled, brightly lit kitchen. There was a bay
window and a built-in breakfast nook with zillions of jigsaw
puzzle pieces strewn on its Formica top: foliage and brick
and shapes that were either slate skies or water.

I sat down, with one socked foot folded under me, and
tried to see if I could make out our trailer from here, but
with the lights on, the windowpanes were as impenetrable
as sheets of mirrored tin.

I stared down at the puzzle pieces.

"You know," Arthur said, bringing over our teacups, "puzzles are one of the best cures I know for insomnia, Kim."

And we talked for a moment about the different ways of combating sleeplessness. Arthur said his late wife used to drink a concoction of warm milk and aspirins which put her right out, while he preferred to come downstairs and play solitaire or fiddle with a puzzle. I said I'd read somewhere about a method (I didn't mention the tabloid) in which the insomniac envisions sleeping on a third side, after trying the two he already has, and this made Arthur laugh. When he laughed, he closed his eyes and a tiny vein on the side of his temple ticked.

Then we fell silent again and Arthur blew on the surface of his tea, as did I, and together we bent our heads over the pandemonium of shapes: without divvying it up or anything, he took on the sky, I the brick and foliage.

But in no time I was despondent again. I couldn't concentrate. I said I was going to take a look at the trailer and I wandered over to the window, cupping my eye against the cold pane.

That's when he did the kindest thing: he extinguished all the kitchen lights so I could see my trailer clearly, and he sat down beside me on the windowsill. I was still holding a piece of foliage, he a shape of sky which he placed on the rim of his saucer like a biscuit.

"You know, it really doesn't look that bad," he said.

The trailer's dented end was facing us; it looked unsalvageable to me.

I didn't say anything.

He stared into the depths of his teacup: you could tell he wasn't sure what to do or say next.

"It's a full moon," he said at last.

I said I guessed it was, then glanced up past yellow street-lamps, over shingled rooftops, through TV antennas, but I couldn't find the moon anywhere.

"There," he said, pointing, and his fingertip eclipsed the moon I had missed, and we sat looking at it, then at its reflection mirrored in the crater of the trailer where it appeared to show, in the dents and dings, all its phases at once—sliver, crescent, quarter and full.

"Kim, I think it's best if you and your mother stay here for a while, until she gets back on her feet."

I asked him if he didn't think we'd be too much trouble.

"Really, after what I've caused? Please." He looked down into his teacup again. "Do you think you're all right now?" he asked.

I said I thought so, and he turned the lights back on. Both of us were a little stunned by the sudden radiance. Then we slid into the breakfast nook again and Arthur showed me a picture of what the puzzle was to become—a brick house with a backdrop of autumn foliage catching the last light of the day—and he asked me to tell him about my mother and me.

I told him where we had lived—Arcadia, Crestline, Thousand Palms, Indian Springs, Oro Grande, and some of the small trailer parks along Route 99 (the names of which I couldn't remember); and I told him where we were heading last night—Indio; and I described some of my mother's high hopes for Indio. Then, opening up even more, I mentioned a little bit about her perfume business.

"Really," he kept saying, but you could see drowsiness was overcoming him again. Once, with his chin on his fist, he all but slipped into oblivion.

I twisted the only button on my pilly cardigan. I said he didn't have to sit up with me.

"Kim, I was only resting my eyes," he said, shaking his head. And we bent over the puzzle once more.

Around three a.m. we got the roof on, and by four, the bright little house was securely locked in place against the puzzled landscape, or maybe this is just a detail I've embellished over the years because what I do remember about that dawn I still see with great clarity: the sky changes from a dark watery violet, to jade, to sepia, to pink, and Arthur sits up with me until the sun emerges, very slowly, behind one of his neighbor's houses.

That was on Saturday (we all slept behind sun-drenched drawn blinds for the better part of the afternoon). On Sunday Arthur explained to my mother and me that he had to unload our trailer so the tow truck could fetch it that afternoon before he returned to work (he designed airplane engines for Hughes Aircraft). I knew she wouldn't want him going in there alone. I grabbed my cardigan, stuffed my nightshirt into my waistband, slipped on my flip-flops, and followed him outside.

"Kim, this isn't necessary. If you're not feeling up to it . . ."

I said my knee didn't even hurt anymore.

Our trailer, catching the morning rays, burned like a sun on his curb. Arthur pried open the screen door and climbed in first. I hesitated for a moment on the aluminum steps, embarrassed by what he might think of us when he saw how we lived.

A green Coke bottle had exploded on the kitchen floor.

The cupboards were flung open and some of our Texaco stemware (fill 'er up, get a free champagne glass) had smashed on the shelves. In the rear, our newspaper curtains had come down and under the sleeping berth, where my mother stored her perfume bottles, a half dozen vials had rolled free. I sat down on the coconut chair and waited to see if Arthur would say anything. He was looking around, taking in the bullet-shaped rooms, the metallic walls, the shattered stemware. Then he crouched down and, picking up a violet-colored vial of my mother's perfume, studied it curiously.

"Ah, so this must be the famous perfume you talked about the other night."

Let's face it—what could he say? For the rest of the day we worked side by side, Arthur in rolled-up shirtsleeves, lugging our belongings into his house, me trailing behind with a pot in one hand, a housecoat in the other. He didn't want me carrying anything heavy.

Sometimes, when he wasn't looking, I'd quickly hide pilfered motel towels, filched restaurant flatware under my mother's slacks or in the deep recesses of our khaki duffel bag. When the trailer was practically dismantled, and Arthur and I were spent, slouched on the last two folding chairs, he suggested I go upstairs and spend some time with my mother.

I dawdled for a moment, asking if I couldn't at least help him sweep up the last of the dregs.

"Kim, she's been alone since noon."

My mother was fast asleep, a *Life* magazine tented over her face. I gently nudged her awake and told her that the tow truck would probably be here anytime now.

She said she wanted to wait by the window. About twenty

minutes later, squinting into the late afternoon sun, we watched as our house and car were winched and cabled to a rig and trundled away in chains.

I started to tell her that everything would be A-okay but she had already fallen asleep on my shoulder. I put her back to bed. I ate the leftover toast on her lunch tray. I leafed through the glossy photos of *Life*. Then, watching the light slowly ebb on the last page, I grew completely despondent again and headed downstairs to see if Arthur wanted to finish the jigsaw puzzle—not to re-create the other night or anything, just for the company.

And there he sat, on the far end of his davenport, with his elbows on his knees, his head in his hands. The blinds were cracked and a last shaft of daylight was falling across our Naugahyde coconut chair, his teak-and-rose breakfront, our pogo-stick pole lamp, the pendants of his chandelier (scattering all their scintillance). To his left sat a stack of my mother's perfume cartons. To his right lay the jumble of our dishes, pots, hangers, Wellingtons, coats, duffel bags, shoe box files, and folding chairs. For a couple of minutes Arthur just looked around. Then, closing his eyes, he slowly let his head sink back into the cushions: I could see that the burden of our being there had finally hit him.

I quietly retreated up the steps.

Whatever Arthur was feeling that afternoon, however, he never let on. Around seven he brought in our dinner trays and plied us with more magazines to read and over the next couple of days, I can't tell you how kind, how gracious he was to us. Each morning, before leaving for his office, he carefully redressed my mother's contusion (attending to her bruise with a lightness of touch that made me realize the full weight of responsibility he felt for causing

her injury), fixed us our breakfast and our lunch, asked if
there was anything we wanted from the grocery store, and
when my mother said she was going stir-crazy lying in bed
all day, he arranged two chaise lounges in his backyard so
we could catch, like sundials, the full orbit of the sun's
rays.

From his tiered yard, we could see the hazy San Fernando
Valley, and the dusty geometry of its streets, and the distant
mountains scrabbling out of the smog, and Arthur's black
Packard as it wended its way down the canyon to work. If
my mother fell asleep (and she slept a lot during those first
couple of days), I'd slip back into the house and begin going
through Arthur's things.

I just wanted to know more about him.

In one bureau drawer, I found a Dutch Masters cigar
box filled with old photographs. They'd clearly been taken
from an album (their corners were sticky with gluey black
felt) and some had faded, as if their subjects had vanished
into sepia and only their souls remained. An elderly couple
hunched stiffly over a ghostly sewing machine : *Mit lieb,
Zayde und Bubbe.* A dark-haired boy in a cowboy suit (Arthur,
I thought). A woman with Arthur's black eyes posing on a
windswept prairie, in a shapeless dress. The elderly couple
again, this time in close-up, peering out of a nest of wrinkles
at Arthur in soldier's fatigues.

In his handkerchief drawer, I came across some Polaroid
snapshots: Arthur and his late blond wife, Arthur embracing
his late blond wife, she in Capri pants, she in a straw hat,
she in a formal gown, in a tube top, and again in a jersey
swimsuit reposing on my chaise lounge.

In the vestibule closet, I unearthed a box of clothes. Each
article had been meticulously folded and swathed in tissue:

a satin nightgown, a black mantilla, a pair of old house slippers. She wore the same size as my mother. For hours afterward, sitting on the lawn, I couldn't get her scent off my hands.

When the shadows of our chaise lounges reached the far end of the cinder-block fence, Arthur would come home. If the winds weren't churning up yet, he'd bring out fresh lemonade and we'd all sip it on the patio, watching dusk fall. The night would be charged with ions. An air raid siren, somewhere in the distance, would begin a test wail, and on the other side of the hills, the shaft of a Hollywood searchlight, announcing a premiere, would slowly spin in a suffusion of dusk and smog, heat and mirage.

Then Arthur and I would fire up the barbecue, or if my mother said she wasn't really hungry, her mood having crashed with the thud of a skyscraper, he'd bring her soup, then come downstairs and patiently explain to me that it was only her concussion, and help me sift through the rubble of her day.

By the end of the first week, I secretly began to harbor a fantasy that even after my mother got better, we could stay on.

Arthur was a widower and my mother was a very attractive woman—thin-boned and blue-eyed and movie-mollish-looking, with a Veronica Lake swagger, and a tincture of world-weary vulnerability—say, Judy Holliday's smoky, lost gaze. Men were constantly drawn to her. She stood five foot eight. And when she was feeling up to it, she wore her hair in the latest fashion—a bouffant, or a flip, or a platinum twist piled up so stiff and fragile it looked as if she'd spun it from light. Plus there was her unique way of seeing the world. It's difficult to put into words exactly but once, during the

course of our travels, even a highway patrolman who en-
countered my mother's view of reality ("Ma'am, you went
through an intersection on a flashing red light." "I went
through on the blink!") drove away astonished.

I hoped Arthur would become as enchanted with her as
some of the other men we'd met along the road.

One afternoon, toward the beginning of our second week,
I spied them standing alone in the kitchen. It was sunset.
Arthur had just come home from work. My mother was
staring out the bay window, her cheek resting against the
cool pane, her blond twist unloosened, gold strands shooting
out like solar flares from the eclipsed outline of her head.

"Gloria," he asked, lightly touching the sleeve of her
nightgown, "is everything okay? Shouldn't you be off your
feet?"

My mother gave a deep sigh. "If I don't get back on the
road again soon, I'm going to lose my perfume empire."

Arthur slowly led her over to the breakfast nook, put up
a kettle for tea, and sat down beside her. He hadn't yet
grasped the full nature of my mother's business. From what
I'd described to him, he still assumed our travels involved
a selling territory of sorts, whereas my mother's business
was a state of mind.

"Gloria, please listen to me. What you're experiencing
right now is just the effects of your concussion. Everything
looks distorted. I'm sure your business isn't falling apart."

"I have a feeling it is. I have a feeling that by the time I
get out there again, my customers will have forgotten me."

My mother's wide-set eyes drifted back to the window.
You must understand that in my mother's mind, her mail
order business really was an empire, the sovereign and be-
nevolent leader of which she always imagined herself.

"Gloria, please, you're not seeing things realistically. I can't imagine anyone, let alone your customers, forgetting you."

"Arthur," she said softly, "you don't know their attention spans."

That night, for the first time, Arthur and my mother sat up talking. I was already in bed and eavesdropped behind a curtain of feigned sleep, carefully cracking open one eye to study the two of them—Arthur suffused in a mixture of eyelash and moonlight, sitting on the edge of our mattress, intently following my mother's stories, she curled in his shadow, her cheek crushed against the white pillow, speaking softly about our past—and as I listened, their voices grew more and more entangled until they entered my dreams . . .

I guess it's time to reveal the secret ingredient in my mother's perfume. In every species there exist scents, precise fragrances called pheromones, that according to my mother's ads, "overwhelm all other senses, allowing the stallion to find that very special filly in the big herd." No one knows if they work in humans (my mother made no written promises) and besides, the scents are so subliminal that even the animal may not know why it's enchanted—ears cocked, tail raised, hooves poised as if ensnared by threads of sudden ardor.

Chapter Three

I t was twelve days, seventeen hours, and eight minutes
into our stay and Arthur had just walked through the front
door. He was standing in his vestibule, briefcase in hand,
copper keys still dangling in the lock (since his wife's ac-
cidental death nearly eight months ago—she'd slipped and
cracked her head in the shower—these first few minutes
in the house were the hardest moments of every day). He
loosened his tie, taking a deep breath to collect himself.
Then, without venturing off his welcome mat, he called our
names. There was a timbre of panic in his voice. We weren't
in any of our familiar haunts—the chaise lounges stood
empty, the hammock still, the bedroom dark. Suddenly he
was frightened that we weren't there, that maybe in his
loneliness he'd made us up, and he began to scan the house.
A lilac glow emanated from his den. It had rained earlier
that day and my mother and I were bathed in the lavender
light of his sunlamp. Our cheeks were flushed and we were
wearing his safety goggles, staring into the opaque orbs,

describing the zigzags of ionic charges and bursting orange nebulae. Arthur had no idea what we were talking about but, at that moment, he really didn't care. He was just grateful to come home and find us, or maybe he was just relieved to find that his house wasn't empty. Wiping his shoes on the mat, he headed up the steps to assure himself that our ultraviolet presence in his life wasn't a mirage.

When he entered the den, my mother and I were still suffused in the otherworldly light. We didn't know he was there. We were chattering away about the tiny universe of lights we saw, about the big one out there, about all my mother's schemes and dreams for our future—moving her perfume empire to the Hawaiian Islands, or Oregon, or dumping the whole enterprise and getting herself a real estate license in Florida. Treading as lightly as he could, Arthur stepped over the rug and leaned against the bookshelves, watching us. Our faces were just inches apart, tilted up toward the sunlamp. Heat, in miragelike waves, ebbed over the surface of my mother's skin. She was now describing the color of phosphenes imploding on her lids. He knew she was a little odd, maybe even mad, but what surprised him was how content he was to come home and just stand within the aura of our warmth. What really worried him was how attached he'd become to our being there. He shut his eyes for a moment, wondering if these out-of-proportion feelings were just a subtle new permutation of his grief. The lamp burned a momentary white ring upon his lids and when he opened them again, my mother and I looked almost alike—the same blond arms, the same long necks, the same oval, slightly asymmetrical faces. Quietly, so as not to seem intrusive, and because, if he was to be honest with himself, he was a little too happy to see us, he slipped out of the den and began dinner.

That night, my mother finally felt well enough to come downstairs to eat. She wore her gold toreador slacks and sombrero earrings and insisted we dine by candlelight, telling Arthur funny anecdotes about some of her perfume customers— Tex, the elderly man who, after cataract surgery, sprayed the stuff on his hospital pillow and claimed he got better treatment from the nurses; Ace, the tattooed marine with ANCHORS and DEATH on his biceps, who purchased half a dozen bottles to make sure that after a date his gals got into something long and flowing (by which my mother was sure he meant a river); Johnny, the boxboy in love with the cashier, who sprayed it on his sleeves one day and finally got her to speak to him (he later confessed to my mother that she'd only told him his sweater was inside out)—and Arthur surprised himself by laughing out loud; normally he didn't like to make light of another person's loneliness. Then I chirped in with a story about exhibiting the perfume at one of my school science fairs (I wanted to be a scientist) and my mother proposed a toast to my winning the Nobel Prize. We all clinked stemware.

Finally my mother said she was exhausted again and bid us good night. We watched her ascend the staircase. Without my mother, Arthur and I fell silent, as if we were waiting for the wake of her powerful presence to subside. Then he proposed dessert and a little television, and suddenly the evening righted itself again. I scooped up our ice cream and followed him over to the big black-and-white Zenith, sprawl-

ing on the rug near his feet. After the first program, however, I too couldn't keep my eyes open and said I was going
to bed. He told me he'd be up in a minute but after I'd gone,
he continued to sit there with his elbows on his knees, his
hands clasped. I waited for him on the first landing, on the
top step, in the green-tiled depths of the bathroom with my
toothbrush in my fist. When he failed to appear, I padded
back to him and quietly sat down by his side.

"Kim, aren't you tired?"

I shook my head.

"You sure?"

I said I was positive.

"You know, you don't have to sit up with me."

I laughed, then fixed my stare on the floor, asking if he
wanted to be alone.

"On the contrary," he said, "on the contrary."

For the next half hour or so, we sat there, side by side
in the TV's jittery light. Just before midnight, when the
station signed off and the target appeared (where it would
remain flickering until dawn), a last commercial came on—
a family at breakfast. And Arthur, who by now looked very
tired, and I, who was exhausted, didn't really grasp what
was being sold: the wax carton of homogenized milk, the
white Frigidaire, the sugary cereal, or the generic family
already beginning to fade on the small screen of our waning
day.

Two days later, basking in a pool of early morning light, I
was sprawled on the living room rug leafing through the
Times when I heard Arthur's footsteps behind me. I intu-

itively stretched out, propped my chin on my fists, and pretended to contemplate the comic strips.

He put his hand very lightly on my hair. And he left it there for just a millisecond longer than a friendly tousle. Just a millisecond, mind you. But I was aware of everything. I was aware of his hand's weight, and its heat, and its texture, I was aware of the very structure of its bones, and the excruciating gentleness with which the pads of his fingertips lay upon my hair.

Then his hand moved and he was ruffling my hair and his shoes retreated and he was gone.

But what remained with me for hours and hours afterward was the tactile weight of his whole being on my head.

After which, every morning, I was either at the bottom of the staircase hunkered on the steps, or up on the top landing leaning over the polished balustrade, or slouched on the living room rug, but every morning I waited for him.

This was our routine: While my mother recuperated upstairs (her purple lump was slowly becoming a lilac shadow), dreaming of getting her perfume empire off the ground again (our trailer and car had come back from the body shop in mint-bright condition), Arthur and I took breakfast together at the Formica breakfast nook, on barstools, facing each other. Then he'd refill our coffee mugs and we'd stroll outside to see what was new in the yard, whether anything had bloomed or died.

Today a fire was burning a couple of hillocks away—it was only a tiny brush fire (the big blazes didn't kick in until the Santa Ana winds blew) but ash and cinder were everywhere. And the air was crackling. And the valley was cloaked in smoke. It had the same kind of beauty that doomsayers evoke when they describe the end of the world.

I sprawled on the grass while Arthur sauntered over to the edge of his property line to see if any fire engines were coming. He stood up on tiptoe, gazing over the cinder-block fence, and I stared at the crenellated imprint left by his black socks on his taut woolly calves.

The streets were empty and after a while, he sat down and together we stared at the flames. He said that when Bel Air caught fire last year, the people threw their jewelry and silverware into their swimming pools to save it. He said that whenever my mother spoke to him about her big-time schemes, that's what he envisioned—a swimming pool filled with bracelets and rings. On the valley floor beneath us, under the gray smoke, I could just make out the dull whack of a tether ball, and children's laughter.

I stretched out on the grass beside him and felt an odd constriction in my chest—not a palpitation or a pounding, just a slight shifting as if my heart had gently rolled on its side, as a sleeper does, and found a more comfortable position, and all at once it occurred to me that it was I who was falling in love with this man.

I slowly got up and padded across the warm grass and the patio bricks and the cool linoleum and the thick carpeted steps. I wanted to talk to my mother. Whatever else may be said about her, she was, after all, my mother.

She was seated at Arthur's walnut wood desk, hunched over a Big Chief tablet, embellishing her customers' sworn testimonials and making up some herself, for a new advertisement blitz, and before I could say anything, she swiveled around in his desk chair and began reading aloud to me some of the letters she'd already composed: one spoke of wanton desire and terrestrial sex, another of the mystery of potions and flesh, a third of an unspeakable hope for love. However loony they sounded, they struck me as truer than anything I could say.

I flopped down on the daybed and buried my face in the tumbled pillows and tried to will myself to sleep but I couldn't let go of consciousness. I heard Arthur's Packard rev up for work, the birds at the feeder, the grind of my mother's pencil sharpener as she cranked out new points. I don't know how many hours I lay there because when I got up again, she was gone. I cracked open the bamboo blinds.

My mother lay sprawled in Arthur's hammock facing the western sky and squinting. It was near dusk and an enormous red sun was sinking into a red landscape: red mountains, red telephone poles, red lawns. Her winged sunglasses, folded and forgotten on her lap, reflected the whole blazing scene in tiny, smoke-tinted detail. There was no breeze, but my mother was in motion anyhow, swinging back and forth, back and forth in the sagging net, propelled by her own internal energy. The ropes of the hammock were taut, practically invisible in the waning light, and my mother, silhouetted against the shimmering red ball of sun, appeared to hover over Arthur's backyard with no visible strings of attachment.

She was staring into space. Unlike her dark glasses, however, my mother's gaze didn't reflect the neighborhood lawns: it burned through them. Below her stretched the hazy San Fernando Valley, due west rose the umber mountains of Tarzana where the fire still smoldered, and beyond that glimmered the cinnamon tile roofs of Malibu Colony. To her right, only three scrub brush mountains away, glittered Hollywood, and to her left, five hours by freeway, pulsed the main artery of the Las Vegas strip. I just knew my mother was chafing to get on the road again and try out her new testimonials.

I snapped the blinds shut. I chewed on a nail for a while. Then I raced to the end of the gravel driveway and waited, like a sentinel, for Arthur to come home. As soon as he pulled in, I told him that my mother was getting antsy, that I thought we'd hit the road again soon.

"Kim, calm down." He cranked open his window. "Are you sure about this? Gloria didn't say anything to me."

I said I was pretty sure.

Arthur closed his eyes for a moment and leaned back, his wing tip shoe on the brake.

"So you're finally leaving," he said.

Then he rolled into the carport but he didn't make any move to cut the engine or get out of his car. His hands remained on the steering wheel, at ten o'clock and two o'clock, and the highbeams continued to burn, boring into the garage wall.

I sat down on the Packard's running board and picked at its rubber treads.

"Kim, did your mother say when?"

I suddenly made up a date. Thursday, June 14. Two days from now.

"I see." He ran his hand through his hair. "Does this have anything to do with the trailer coming back? I mean, does Gloria know you can both stay longer if you like?"

I hurried around to the passenger side and climbed in beside him. I said I didn't know if she knew that.

He tapped on the wheel. "Damn. I should have made that clearer."

The highbeams were ricocheting off the rafters, blanching his face: I couldn't read his expression.

"You're absolutely sure about Thursday? I mean, Gloria changes her mind an awful lot."

I said I was sure.

"Well, I guess it's all set then," he said, clearing his throat and killing the motor.

He gathered up his briefcase and I followed him inside. I don't know what I expected him to do but all he did was what he normally does upon coming home—he wiped his shoes on the mat, he brought my mother some lemonade, he began tidying up the odds and ends we'd left in the wake of our day: a lipstick-stained coffee cup, her pop-over housecoat, a plum pit in an ashtray. When the living room was straightened up, he swept out the foyer. Then he trudged over to the hall closet and lugged out the Hoover and all its attachments—floor nozzles, dusting brushes, hoses and wands—even though he normally vacuumed only on Sundays. He started in one corner and fastidiously worked his way across the shag carpeting, up and down the staircase, between the balusters, under the furniture, behind the breakfront, even along the lip of the window sashes. When the machine finally sputtered and the bag was full—I mean, it couldn't take another dust ball—he toted the lumbering contraption into the kitchen and was in the act of emptying it when the unwieldy bag slipped from his hands, releasing a mushroom cloud of dust. For a couple of minutes he just looked at it. Then he picked up the bag by its rubber throat and hurled it across the room.

I was standing behind the Dutch doors. The lights were off. I don't think he saw me.

Turning away, he rooted his hands in his pockets and stared out at the blackness beyond the meshing of the screen door. He looked very sad. A breeze wafted in. He shivered.

I could see the outline of his fists in his pockets. After a while, he turned back to the mess again and, dragging out the whisk broom and the dustpan, meticulously swept up every last speck. Then he sat down at the breakfast nook, put his elbows on the table and removed a piece of lint from his shirtsleeve, and another and another and another.

It was very dark. The only light came from the oven clock, bathing Arthur in its radium-green glow. I quietly sat down beside him. He was staring at his hands.

"I just wish you weren't leaving."

The anomaly of childhood is that despite its brevity, child-hood takes up a lot of square footage in memory's tight quarters. I think this is because the furniture and rooms in those early years are remembered as enormous. That evening Arthur looked small and vulnerable sitting alone at one end of his sectional davenport clasping and unclasping his hands, or pacing back and forth in his book-lined den. Sometime around midnight he came into our room. My mother had just fallen asleep, her legs dreamily entwined. I was pre-tending to be out, under the moon-cold sheets.

"Gloria," he whispered, sitting down on the edge of our bed.

My mother stirred.

"I've been thinking, there's no reason on earth why you can't run your business from here."

My mother blinked open her sleep-crumpled eyes.

"Use my living room as your headquarters. I don't mind."

My mother shook herself awake and slowly arose, wrap-ping her nightgown around her.

"And let's talk about Kim for a moment," Arthur was saying.

I was listening very closely now.

"She only has a year or so of high school left. Gloria, she said she wants to be a scientist. If you stay, I think it would give her the kind of stability she needs to get into college. After that, we could just play things by ear. I don't care, Gloria."

He was looking away from her, at his hands, at the stippled shadows cast on them by the bamboo blinds.

"This is very difficult for me to put into words, but I've been so . . . so happy since you and Kim moved in. I don't want you to leave."

Chapter Four

To my astonishment, my mother agreed to stay. Next morning she sat with Arthur on the steps of our trailer talking until close to noon. I knew she was doing this for me, and there was something heartbreaking about her posture: the resigned way she toyed with the handle of his briefcase and tried to concentrate, the way she couldn't sit still, interminably winding a blond wisp around her finger and glancing off past the hem of his driveway.

Finally Arthur patted her hand and said he really had to leave for work.

My mother sighed, and stood up, and watched him drive off. Then she slowly pivoted around and stared at her reflection in the mint-bright trailer. The sun was above her and she had to squint to see herself—slippered and robed and standing on a suburban driveway. Biting her lip, she turned away and clopped up the front walk to me, while another Gloria, her mirrored image, also bit her lip and turned away, clopping into the depths of the trailer.

For the next few weeks she tried to make a stab at stability. She drove me down to the local high school and registered me for the fall semester. She even offered to take in Arthur's dry cleaning, water the lawn, do the grocery shopping, at least until her business really got going again. But I could see she was out of her element. After the first week or so, I found the lawn parched, Arthur's shirts balled in the trunk, the grocery cart abandoned near the tabloid racks (a single carton of ice cream sweating in the basket) while she checked out how her competition was doing.

One Saturday, Arthur surprised her by bringing home a brand-new desk for her—a modern teak affair with tubular metal legs and streamlined drawers. My mother pulled up a folding chair and just stared and stared at it, running her finger over its polished lip, rolling its drawers in and out, in and out on their steel ball bearings. Setting her hands very lightly upon its work surface, as if touching piano keys, she looked up at Arthur with befuddled gratitude and told him how incredibly touched she was by his unflagging belief in her.

That night under the chandelier, her elbows on the desk, her cheek on her fist, she composed the first advertisement for her new comeback campaign: a combination of home pickup (for those last-minute dates) and/or mail order. Arthur leaned over her shoulder and corrected her spelling. I watched them both from my solitary perch on the sofa arm.

And a week later, she in turn surprised Arthur with a Hawaiian Tiki for his front yard, explaining how it was the latest rage in lawn decorations. Plus, she said, when her customers started coming by the house, it would give them a landmark to find rather than just a pale address stenciled on the dusty curb.

But her customers didn't come. Fridays (usually her top selling day) one or two old regulars dropped by, ringing Arthur's doorbell, commenting on how much Gloria had come up in the world. But that was all.

Now a secret must be imparted: even prior to the accident, my mother's business wasn't doing that well. Whether her ads no longer worked or her territories had dried up or there were just a limited number of lonely men who hoped beyond logic and reason for love, I can't say. By the time Arthur had rolled into our lives, we were barely making ends meet. Unfortunately my mother didn't like to remember this (in times of stress, she preferred an abridged past) and as one unsuccessful day faded into another, all she could think about was our future. While she mulled over her prospects, spending more and more time by herself, slung in the hammock or taking long drives through the hills, I was pretty much left alone with Arthur.

And this is what took place: Saturday afternoon. Four p.m. Arthur was napping in his armchair, having just mowed the lawn. I was padding toward him from the linoleum depths of the laundry room. Between us a perfect diagonal of light crossed the living room, the air mad with dust. The blood in my ears pounded. Crouching down by his feet, I lightly printed in the dust on the glass end table, just inches to the left of his oblivious hand, the words LOVE ME. Then I wiped them out with my palm, and carefully, so as not to let my breath pass over his wrist, I blew the evidence away. Or I would come upon Arthur leaving the bathroom, the tiles still damp from his shower. I'd close the door behind me, snap the lock, jiggle the handle to make sure it was fastened, peel off my T-shirt, unhook my bra, step out of my jeans, and stand naked before the mirror scrutinizing myself through the fog of what I imagined his breath had left on the glass. Or I'd be hanging out on the front lawn, waiting for Arthur to come home, fretting about how to confess my feelings to him when I'd suddenly see my mother pull in, her eyes blank, her arm idly dangling out the driver's window, and I'd know it was her I should be worrying about.

She wasn't doing too well. Two weeks passed with only one sale. And she wouldn't talk to me about it. Most mornings she just sat at her desk, staring into her coffee cup. Up until now, when things weren't going well for her, we'd just take off. I didn't know how to handle this. So one night, the moment she dropped off to sleep, I slipped out of our bed and went to find Arthur.

His den light was on, but he too was asleep, his head resting on his desk, a blueprint of an airplane engine creased beneath his cheek. For a moment, standing above him, the French curves, flywheels, and propellers looked to me like a dream that had bloomed from his head. I gingerly touched his shoulder and he blinked open his eyes.

"Was I sleeping?"

I nodded.

"I dreamt I was building an airplane engine out of rubber bands."

I apologized for waking him. I said I wanted to talk to him while my mother was asleep. I said I was terribly worried about her. Sitting down on the rug by his slippered feet, I told him that my mother's business wasn't exactly booming—

"Kim, I already guessed as much."

But what really worried me was her listlessness. She'd never had to work things out by staying in one place before.

"Does this have anything to do with money, Kim? If Gloria's worried about money, she shouldn't be—"

I shook my head.

"Are you sure? Because I could explain to your mother that she doesn't need to work. Really, I make enough money for all of us."

"Arthur," I said, "that would be the worst thing for her." I described how once, when we were flat broke, she threw our last quarter into the wishing well at Caesars Palace, convinced that something grander would come from the splash. I said my mother lived for those splashes.

"Kim, listen to me. I want to help. I just don't understand what you want me to do."

I said I thought he could talk to her. My mother truly respected him. Maybe he could get her to think about going into another line of work, or finding new products to market.

"Kim, your mother loves her perfume business."

"I know that. But what she loves about—" I stared down at the rug to the left of his slippered foot. Even in my peripheral vision, I could make out the packed muscle of his calf, and his ankle, and the curve of his heel as it tapered into his lambskin slipper. I was only fifteen and completely in love with this man and I knew that if I talked about love in any form, even my mother's love for her business, I'd tell him about the printed messages I'd left for him in the dust, about the showers and the fog and my naked self. I said, "Arthur, my mother's real forte isn't running her business. Over the years she's had dozens of businesses, sold everything from Geiger counters to weight loss potions. Her real forte is dreaming her businesses up." I followed the crease in his pant leg up to his knee. "That's when she's happiest, when she first comes up with the ideas, when she's still

projecting her profits, when—" And here I didn't quite have
the language to describe it: when her dreams were still being
erected before they had to buckle to fit into reality.

I asked him if he could talk to her tonight.

"She's asleep."

"I know my mother. She won't mind being woken up."

"Kim, I can't—"

"Arthur, please. I'm worried she's going to want to take
off again. I don't think she can handle another day."

He patted my head, then rose to his feet and scuffed into
our bedroom.

"Hey," he said, touching my mother's shoulder.

She looked up at him, tasted her lips, and rose amid the
sheets, resting her temple lightly on his arm.

"Kim said it would be all right to wake you."

"I wasn't really asleep," she said, using a corner of the
sheet to rub her eyes.

"Gloria, I gather your business isn't going well right now."

She shrugged. "It's more complicated than that. I
feel . . . I don't know . . . unneeded." And she rested the
full weight of her head on his shoulder. He put his arm
around her.

I watched them from the dark hallway. Finally, I said I
was going downstairs to sleep on the couch.

I closed the door to give them privacy, then sat down on
the top landing, then on the cold windowsill, before crashing
onto the sofa. I didn't go to sleep. I stared intently at the
ceiling, listening for the sound of Arthur's footsteps as he
padded back to his room, but it didn't come.

In the morning, my mother seemed to feel a lot better.
She talked about expanding her business, teased Arthur
about becoming her partner, fixed his tie when he knotted

it crookedly, and thanked him for being so patient with her. He'd really said some things that hit home. Maybe the accident had thrown her for a bigger loop than she thought? Maybe she wasn't thinking "long term" enough? While she buttered herself a third piece of toast, I sat hunched in the breakfast nook, staring into my cereal bowl. Arthur kept his eyes trained on the slow-burning ashes of his cigarette.

That afternoon my mother asked him to drive her downtown to the main newsstand so she could pick up some foreign magazines and a half dozen tabloids (I sat in the back seat; I didn't want them out of my sight). She wanted to check out what products weren't being marketed in the States yet, or if they were being sold, which products weren't being marketed creatively. As soon as we got home, she flopped onto the sofa beside him, with one slippered foot folded under her, poring over them. I made sure I sat on his other side, squeezed between his thigh and the armrest.

That night my mother didn't sleep with Arthur or me; she sat up reading her magazines.

Many of the products advertised, and the claims made for them, were complete scams, she told Arthur the next morning. These truly irked her because they ruined entrepreneurship for everyone else. Others, as interesting as they sounded on paper, were just too difficult to market (i.e., the alpha wave brain machine that was supposed to have you meditating like a Zen monk in twenty-two minutes). She didn't feel her particular clientele would go in for transcendence. A few products, however, did strike her as possibilities and over the course of the weekend, she jotted down, scratched out, rewrote, and asked Arthur his opinion of a whole list of potential goods: a treadmill for dog owners who were too lazy to walk their pets, a home face-lift kit, a home bomb shelter kit, Vitamin Q, a passive exercise machine, and—

"Here's one for the books," she said, wandering late Sunday night into the kitchen where Arthur and I sat playing cards. "This is exactly the kind of hokey entrepreneurship I was trying to tell you about."

And she read us a tiny article from one of the tabloids:

> Pyramid Parties are back! From every stratum of society men and women are secretly gathering in Quality Inns, Motel 6s, even posh hotels, to play Pyramid, a strictly adult game that is fast becoming the rage for anyone willing to risk $1,500 for the promise of a $10,000 payoff.
>
> Here's how it works: Each "pyramid" starts with a "pivotal stone," the organizer, and six "boulders," the initial investors. If the stone and the boulders can recruit eight "rocks" willing to plunk down $1,500, the pivotal stone takes the profits and rolls away. The boulders become stones, the rocks become boulders, and everyone tries to dig enough "raw material" willing to bet that the pyramid will last long enough for them to reach the top.

My mother folded up the paper and shook her head. "Can you believe it?" she asked.

"Gloria," Arthur said, laying down his cards (he almost had gin rummy), "I've got to be perfectly honest with you. I don't understand how you can say that pyramids are 'hokey' and Vitamin Q isn't. Maybe I'm missing something but I just don't get it."

My mother slid into the breakfast nook beside him.

"To begin with," she explained, "Vitamin Q has just been discovered. No one knows if it works. Whereas pyramid schemes are as old as the hills. It's only a glorified chain letter. I mean, really, if you're going to pull a stunt like this, at least come up with a fresh approach. It's this type of shoddy marketing that drags down the whole profession."

And she wandered back into our bedroom. I stayed up with Arthur.

About a week later, as lost as ever (none of her ideas were panning out), she was standing in the supermarket studying the racks of new tabloids, her public research facilities, when she thought she overheard the word "pyramid." She looked up, blinking. To her left stood trays of chewing gum, and breath mints, and almond and chocolate candy bars; to her right a stack of copper-topped batteries. The checker was weighing a silver-haired lady's red apple on a stainless steel scale. My mother glanced down again. "Last Thursday," she distinctly heard the old lady whisper to the checker, "I became a stone." For a couple of minutes my mother continued to stand there, motionless, pretending to read this week's lurid headline, but seeing nothing—not the old woman's cereal box, or her pea soup can, or her Red Delicious apple as they drifted by on the rubber conveyor belt.

Next, while pushing a grocery cart back to her car, my mother thought she spied a brand-new Cadillac idling beside her dusty convertible. Normally only Chevrolets and Fords were parked in this lot. My mother stopped and squinted over the car roofs, curious to see who was inside the Caddy, but all she could make out, as the sleek machine glided away, was a silver-haired profile biting into a red apple behind the scintillating diamond of sunlight reflected in the rear window.

Four days later (you must understand, these incidents were leaving their mark on my mother's impressionable brain), while slung in Arthur's hammock, pondering what to do about her future, she was jarred back to reality by a burst of laughter filtering through the cinder-block fence. Some neighborhood ladies were playing bridge in the adjacent backyard. My mother was about to cover her ears when, amid the titters and murmurs that reached her, she overheard a hoarse voice announce: "My Bible group is going pagan, ladies—we're about to start our own pyramid." Quietly, my mother slipped out of the taut net and inched closer to the fence. She could only make out whispering now but the buzz that reached her intrigued her because it was whispering.

"Arthur," she said the instant he came home from work, "I feel as though something big is going on out there without me."

She told him about the women next door and what she'd overheard in the backyard, and about the silver-haired lady and what she'd overheard in the supermarket. Then, catching her breath, she described the brand-new Cadillac and the red apple.

"Gloria," Arthur said, "I don't know what you heard next door, but seeing an old woman buy an apple in the grocery store and then later seeing someone with gray hair eating an apple in a Cadillac doesn't necessarily mean it's the same person. It may just be a coincidence."

My mother sat down on the windowsill and sighed. It was impossible to tell whether she was looking out at the horizon or deep inside herself.

"Arthur," she said softly, "coincidences are all we mortals get to compose our own lives."

In my mother's defense, it was true that during those first hot weeks in August, all anyone seemed to be talking about were pyramid parties. You couldn't click on the TV, or push a radio button, or flip open the newspaper without encountering another story about a housewife in Azusa or a retired plumber in Panorama City who had made their way to the top of a pyramid and rolled off with a fortune.

And on top of that, my mother wasn't sleeping too well. Late at night, whenever I felt her stir from our bed, I followed only to find her standing alone on the dark patio, perfectly still, unblinking. All around her the wind blew, and the neighbors' pools plashed, and the house creaked, and dry leaves scuttled over her bare feet. Without looking down, she'd lift up her leg and sway, flamingo-like in her wind-rippled pink nightie, scratching her instep with her ravenously bitten fingernails, but never once taking her eyes off the dusky metropolis spread out on the valley floor beneath her.

"What is happening to me?" she asked us over breakfast. "What is going on? I used to have my finger on the pulse of America . . . well, maybe not America but at least Southern California and Nevada. I used to have a vision of what the public wanted. Oh, I'm not saying in any big-time way like Walt Disney or Howard Hughes or anything. But, guys, I should have seen the pyramids coming. I should have been ready with a plan of my own."

"Gloria," Arthur said, pouring himself a third cup of coffee, "I don't mean to be presumptuous, but if it was me and I was so obsessed—"

"I am not obsessed," my mother corrected him, "I'm preoccupied."

"All right, preoccupied then. Anyway, what I'm trying to say is this: If the pyramids mean so much to you, why don't you just join one and stop kicking yourself for not having thought them up? Indulge. You don't have to risk fifteen hundred dollars. If you'd like, I'll call Mrs. Talbot next door and ask if you can sign up for her one-hundred dollar one."

"Never," my mother said.

Arthur sighed, shaking his head. "Gloria, you said so yourself—everybody knows it's a scam. Just have a little fun!"

"Don't you understand? It's not the concept of the pyramids I morally object to," my mother explained, "it's the packaging."

She put down her fork, wiped her lips with her paper napkin, placed her elbows up on the plastic-topped table, and leaned over her yolk-stained plate.

"When Kim was just a toddler," she began, "long before I started my perfume empire, I used to be in the health and beauty field. Do you remember those days at all, Kim?"

I glanced up at Arthur. We were sitting across from each other. I touched his ankle with my socked foot and shrugged.

"Well, we were just starting out," my mother continued. "I was no more than a kid myself. Anyhow, the two of us used to tool around to all the beauty conventions and state fairs selling our wares. At the time, I had an exclusive on a product called Dreamaway. It was some sort of solvent you added to your bath at night and in the morning you were supposed to awaken four, maybe five pounds thinner. Kim and I lugged this portable tub everywhere. I used to let her play in it during off-hours with her little rubber ducks and balls. Of course, sans solvent. I mean, don't take me wrong, I was pretty sure the stuff didn't work but if I was wrong, Kimmy was just a tiny rail in those years and after a couple of baths, who knows, she might have vanished. And I was crazy about the kid.

"Anyway, one day, in the booth across the way, these two musclemen were setting up their barbell equipment—a whole medieval torture rack—while Kim and I were pouring the last buckets of hot water into our tub, and as the convention doors opened, I lifted Kimmy onto my lap and I said, 'Look, pumpkin, on one side of the aisle is reality'—I pointed to the barbells—'and on the other side is a dream'—I pointed to our tub. 'Let's see what the American public wants!' It's the dream I sell, Arthur. That is my calling in life."

Arthur didn't say anything. He continued slowly eating his eggs, taking a swig of coffee from time to time.

"Okay," my mother went on, "let's take a packaging concept that's closer to home, something related to your own field, Arthur. What is the difference between the engineering design of a Cadillac and the design of a Ford?"

"Gloria, is this a rhetorical question or do you really want me to answer it?"

My mother looked surprised. "I really want you to answer it," she said.

"All right, a Cadillac has a V-eight engine and—"

"Wings," she said. "The difference between a Cadillac and a Ford is that the tail fins on the Caddy are designed to look like wings and create the illusion of flight. For those extra bucks, what you buy when you purchase a Cadillac is the dream that this time you are really taking off and getting somewhere in life."

Then my mother quietly finished her coffee, stretched, buttered herself another piece of toast and didn't mention the pyramids again.

But later that day I sensed something was up. She told us that she was going out for a spin but she only drove to

the low stone parapet at the far end of the cul-de-sac and
parked the car facing west. Rain clouds were advancing
across the valley. Her window was cranked down so I could
see her clearly from the front porch (all the other glass in
the car had turned opaque, reflecting the black convolutions
rolling toward her), and there she sat, framed in the driver's
window, for what seemed like hours, her fist on the top of
her steering wheel, her chin on her fist.

Then, making a three-point turn, she gunned the engine
a couple of times and sped off. Three hours later, after
driving aimlessly around in the storm, while idling next to
a car wash, where these things normally don't take place,
my mother had an illumination—not unlike the visions
saints see in their waking dreams. The sun was out again,
her windshield was streaked and dirty, and through the
prismatic arcs left by her wipers, she saw a row of driverless
cars rolling into a celestial mist. She lined up behind them,
paid the attendant, lowered her antenna, cranked up her
windows, glided onto the conveyor belt, relinquished control
of her steering wheel, and allowed herself to be passively
led inside. Drops of water began to bang and thump on her
roof and then clouds of soap flakes splattered against her
windshield, and enormous brushes churned them all to suds,
and the world was suds and then the world was legible and
clean and she emerged into the sunlight: bumpers steamed,
tail fins turned iridescent. She'd passed through walls of
water, flash floods, hot winds. It was then and there, on
the parking lot of a car wash, in broad daylight, while the
attendant blotted the last drops from her windshield, that
my mother conceived of a fresh way to market the pyramids.

"Arthur," she said as soon as she walked through the
front door, "do you remember those movies where an air-

plane takes off in bad weather and the pilot is knocked unconscious and the copilot has a heart attack and the stewardess has to take control of the storm-tossed plane? And the clouds are so thick she can't even see her own wings? And she doesn't know where she is or where she's going? And suddenly she makes that leap of faith and guides the plane and its passengers to safety and although, of course, they never show it on the *big screen,* she guides her own life to inevitable fame and wealth? Arthur, I experienced something of that vision today."

My mother took a deep breath, patted her damp brow with her wrist, and explained her concept.

"There will be an 'airplane,' Arthur, just waiting to take off. When every 'ticket' is sold, when the 'flight' is full, the pilot will pocket the fares and bail out. The copilot will take the controls, the stewardesses will become copilots, the passengers will become crew members, and all everyone has to do is find more passengers willing to gamble that the flight will last long enough for them to finally take off in life. As one of our first passengers, Arthur, you'll immediately be promoted to navigator."

Arthur laughed. "I have a lousy sense of direction. These things never work out for me."

"Concentrate on where you're going, Arthur, not on where you've been. I am the pilot. You can be the copilot if you like."

Arthur perched on the sofa's armrest and slowly massaged his temples. "Do you really think anyone else will want to get on board?"

"There is a passenger born every minute!" my mother said.

She traipsed over to the windows, swept aside the curtains and gazed out.

"When I think that I came up with this all on my own, even I'm astonished."

She said she had to sit down.

"Arthur," she continued, sinking into his recliner, her feet raised on the hassock, "everybody's investing in the pyramids. Why not my airplane? Even Mrs. Talbot next door has confessed that she'd dipped into her little white church purse. I'm sure I could convince her, and all the rest of her Bible group, to bail out of that pagan pyramid and climb on board my plane."

Then she touched the release knob and jettisoned herself out of the recliner.

"I'll tell them they're buying tickets on Revelation Airlines. I'll throw a 'takeoff' party at a swanky hotel. They'll probably ascend without the plane!"

"Gloria," Arthur said quietly, taking her by her shoulders, "now listen to me. I'm going to be perfectly frank with you. I just don't understand how your airplane scheme really differs from the pyramid scheme."

My mother rolled her eyes, sighed loudly, shook her head in disbelief.

"I can't believe you don't see the difference!"

She sat Arthur down.

"Okay, close your eyes and tell me what you think of when I say 'pyramid.' "

Arthur closed his eyes. "I see golden sands," he said, "and I see camels, and an oasis with swaying palms—"

"Well," my mother interrupted him, slamming her eyes shut, "when I think of 'pyramids,' I see exhausted slaves dragging their illusions across a parched desert by fraying hopes. But when I think of 'airplanes,' I see uncharted skies and broken sound barriers and heroes in silver jumpsuits."

She caught her breath.

"Arthur, I am not dealing with the banal arithmetic of earning a couple of bucks, I am dealing with the aerodynamics of human dreams."

Chapter Five

That evening my mother was too excited to eat her dinner and went to bed early (if she was about to peddle dreams, what better way than sleep for her to prepare herself?). Arthur and I sat across from each other at the dining room table, he absently toying with his paper napkin, me using the prongs of my fork to poke at my untouched pudding.

"You know," he said finally, "I almost wish your mother would take up her perfume business again."

I stopped what I was doing. "Please don't get involved," I said.

We were eating by candlelight (my touch) and I really couldn't see him through the almond-shaped flames.

"Her scheme's pretty harmless, Kim. I can't imagine anyone signing up for it. Besides, by tomorrow morning, she'll probably be on to something new."

I said I didn't think so. I said this wasn't the first time she'd gotten obsessed by an idea. And I told him about the time she tried selling lakefront desert property and about last year's dream of franchising metal detectors on Redondo Beach.

"Kim, please, I understand."

I stared down at my sneakers, then at my hands, then into the candle's nervous flame dodging on the wick. I said I just didn't want him to get involved, was all.

"Hey, cheer up, you never know—maybe she'll hit it big this time and finally get what she wants. Although I have to admit, I'm not quite sure I know what it is your mother wants. A mansion? A swimming pool?" He started to clear the table, scraping off our plates. "Kim, are you okay?"

I nodded. I said I just wanted to sit for a while. Then I snuffed out the candles and watched the smoke rise. There was no way to explain to Arthur that for my mother this dream, like all her others, wouldn't end until her descent. She wouldn't stop until she saw herself bailing out of the silver airplane, her wind-chapped fists tightened around the big bucks. My mother didn't care about a bigger house or a swimming pool. Possessions, in point of fact, held no interest whatsoever for her. What my mother was after, had always been after, was something outside of material gain, something that rendered the big house empty, the pool drained of meaning. I'd seen my mother standing in front of a gumball machine with prizes, as transfixed by the plastic jewelry, squirt guns, and jawbreakers as Cortés was by the Aztecs' gold. Obviously, at forty-four years old, it was inconsequential to her what the machine would expel, a tutti-frutti sucker or a brass ring. Yet each time she dropped another copper penny into the slot, her breath caught. What my mother was experiencing in the guise of a gumball machine, why her palms turned clammy each and every time she twirled the knob, was exactly why she'd concocted her airplane scheme. She lived, dreamed, and breathed for those exalted moments between the promise and the prize.

As soon as I heard Arthur start the dishes, I headed upstairs. I was determined to keep her from involving him. She was sleeping on her back, her arms folded across her chest. I stretched across the sheets and put my head on her lap. Blinking sluggishly, she shook herself free of her dream.

"I'm sorry I woke you," I lied.

"Hey, it's okay, darling," she murmured, enveloping me in her arms. She said she wanted to get up anyhow—the middle of the night was her best time to start planning things.

"Mom, listen to me"—I could feel, by the rhythm of her breathing, that I had her attention. I started to tell her about Arthur and me but since there was nothing really to tell, I just lay there, my head rising and falling with her breath.

She slowly wound one of my curls around her fingers. "Honey?" she asked.

"Mom, I really, really like Arthur," I said.

"Honey, I know you do. So do I. That's why I'm including him on the ground floor of my plan."

"Don't."

"Kimmy, I couldn't do that to him. Listen," she whispered, kissing my brow—suddenly I had the forlorn sensation that we were two discrete beings occupying the same bed, our bodies entwined but our minds cartwheeling off in different directions—"I know it's a little too soon to be predicting anything, but this time, this time, I really think we're going to make it, darling."

. . .

My mother never looked more beautiful than when she was preparing for a scheme. Over the next couple of days, she didn't run an errand, or drop by tabloid racks, or fill up her gas tank without encountering—well, not exactly prepaying passengers, but honest hardworking men and women definitely interested in hearing more about her "takeoff" party. If these people were tempted by my mother's schemes, it's not because they were particularly gullible. There exist rare individuals (Mom being one of them) who, by a quirk of creation, act as natural conductors through which the vague longings of the rest of us are transformed into abject needs. Had she only chosen to sell something tangible—houses, cars, treasury bonds—there's no telling how far she might have gotten in this world.

According to her calculations, there were four ingredients that made up any successful entrepreneurial campaign: a good idea, experience, a practical workaday strategy, and an unknown factor—let's call it ingredient X or the heightened sense of possibilities.

The first thing she did was scout around for a hotel suite with the right ambience for her takeoff party. She would have preferred a hotel with marble statuary and a plush lobby where the bellhops wear silver buttons on cardinal-red uniforms, but she settled for a centrally located Holiday Inn.

Next she wrote to all her old perfume customers inviting them to attend her party and climb on board her plane.

Then she got on the horn and talked it up to all her mail order cronies (as world-weary as these schemers acted, they were usually the first to sign up for one another's scams.

You see, in truth, they really did believe in their work.)

Finally she hit the streets to get the word of mouth out and make personal pitches to any of her former customers who seemed interested. Sometimes she'd disappear for a whole day. Other times she'd ask me to come with her. I remember one afternoon feeling my old pride in her as I listened to her give her takeoff spiel to one of her regulars in a sweltering laundromat. Simultaneously I became overwhelmed by an unbearable sadness as I watched his socks and shirts, pants and sneakers falling, falling, falling past the portholes of the dryers—I knew deep down her airplane scheme would never fly.

In the evenings, as the big day drew near, she spent more and more time with Arthur. She asked him to draw her a picture of an airplane for a promotional handbill. She wanted to know when he'd sign on. She needed to run a few new ideas by him. She had to have his opinion of this and that. It seemed like I never got to be alone with him anymore.

On Friday night, forty-eight hours before her big blast-off, while she was making last-minute phone calls, I scouted the whole house for him—upstairs, downstairs, laundry room, and yard. Finally, I spied the garage light burning. Arthur was sitting on his Packard's running board, absently picking some mud off the fender. I sat down beside him. I really had nothing to say, I just wanted to be near him.

"Are you going to sign up?" I asked, only to break the silence.

Arthur stopped what he was doing. I could see the vein on the side of his temple jump.

"Kim, please! Your mother asks me that every five minutes!"

I sighed deeply (very much like my mother) and scuffed over to the garage door, pushing the automatic opener. I said I was sorry to have disturbed him. I said I didn't know he needed all his concentration to clean his car.

A square of garage light, like a slowly moving eclipse, rolled down the driveway.

"Kimberly, stop, I'm sorry. Your mother's driving me a little nuts, is all."

And he walked out into the night with me. We sat down on a couple of rocks, near the Hawaiian Tiki.

"So," I asked, poking at the grass with a twig, "are you going to sign up?"

"I don't know."

"I just don't think you should encourage her," I said.

"Kim, what difference does it make if I give your mother money or pretend I'm buying a ticket for her cockamamy airplane ride? You know I'd give her whatever she needed anyway."

A rag of white clouds passed overhead. Moths were wheeling around the streetlights. Across the cul-de-sac, vapor rose on a sprinklered lawn.

"I just wish things were like they used to be," I mumbled, "when you spent more time with me."

A breeze kicked up, blowing spray our way. I shivered and wrapped my arms around my knees.

"Are you cold?" he asked softly.

I shrugged and he switched over to my rock, putting his arm around me.

"Do you want to go in?"

"Not really," I said.

And he continued to sit with me, on the same granite boulder, for quite some time. We watched Mr. Talbot drag his trash cans to the curb. Then Mrs. Talbot shut off the sprinklers, leaving the lawn gleaming with dew. On the valley floor beneath us, banks of store lights began going out, and the big orange above the Orange Julius stopped spinning, and there was only an occasional whoosh of traffic. Finally Arthur suggested we get some sleep and we trudged upstairs. In the living room, my mother's desk lamp was still burning.

The night before the takeoff party, my mother was exhausted from attending to every last detail for her airplane's success but she was too tense to fall asleep. Collapsing on Arthur's davenport, she closed her eyes for a sec, put her feet up on the cushions, and tried to conjure up an image that has always relaxed her. She envisions a silver charm swinging on a bright chain and a child's unlined palm grappling to hold it (she knows the palm to be her own before time and loss and life have etched it). Then she and the child enter the antechamber of sleep and everything comes back to her in vivid colors. She recognizes her blue grammar school tunic, its pleats and wafer-size buttons, and her white anklets and black patent leather Mary Jane shoes, which reflect on their polished tops herself at seven years old and the silver charm she's reaching for. She is receiving a prize from the principal of her elementary school in Laval, Quebec, for best attendance in her first-grade class and once again, almost thirty-eight years later, she experiences the truly satiating feeling of being recognized and rewarded for all her diligence and dogged hard work. Then the charm topples into her palm and she nods off. . . .

In the meantime, Arthur was upstairs, also on the brink

of sleep. Worn out from having helped my mother all Saturday, he was stretched out on his sofa bed in his white shirt and slacks. For a couple of minutes, he could almost hear my mother's voice again—not her actual words, just the lilting murmur of her talk mingling with the roar of a jet engine he'd tested at work that week. And he recalled an earache he'd once had, hammering in his head like a piston, and his wife pressing warm salves to his ear and reciting nonsense poetry to him. He wanted to be married again more than anything else. He draped his arm over his eyes and thought about my mother again. He still didn't have the slightest idea of who she was, even after he'd slept with her; the woman was completely elusive. Once she'd fixated on her mad scheme, he couldn't get her to talk about anything else. He rolled over on his stomach and pressed his face against the warm cushions and remembered how, as a boy, pressing himself against warm tiles after swimming, he'd draw the silhouette of a woman on the hot cement with the chlorinated water, then stretch out inside that woman until she evaporated—and that was what making love to Gloria had been like. He turned over on his side and tried to envision his wife's face, found he couldn't, and felt a surge of panic. A car sped by. He saw a twin-engine turboprop banking away from him with a hybrid of my mother and me and his wife at the controls: her face turned to the sunset, scorched, her hair on fire. A salty tear burned under his eyelids and he thought, "This is enough, you must get ahold of yourself and decide what to do." Then his fingers lost their grip on consciousness and he plunged into sleep.

I was also in bed, two doors away from Arthur, but I was fully conscious, trying to imagine what he looked like coming out of the shower. I could visualize the steam, and the tub's frosted curtain, and Arthur's vague shape scattered over its foggy pleats, but that was all. It seemed to me that if I could just see him clearly, despite the steam and the opaque curtain, my need for him would supersede my mother's and he wouldn't get involved in her scheme tomorrow. I rolled over on my side and tried to will him to come to me—not his specter but Arthur himself. And when he failed to appear, no matter how hard I concentrated, I climbed out of bed, tiptoed downstairs, checked to see that my mother was asleep, crept back up, slipped across the hall, and entered Arthur's room.

He was sleeping on his side, his left arm embracing his pillow, his white shirt penciled in gray light. The moon was diffused by fog. I turned on his desk lamp, carefully positioned myself within its halo of light, and unbuttoned my blouse.

I could no longer see Arthur. He was just outside the rings of luminosity, but I sensed he was fully awake now. I slipped my left arm out of my sleeve, then my right.

I could make out his books, and the brass casters of his sofa bed, and within the sofa's shadowed cushions, his silhouette, taut and still.

I had no plot or plan: I just wanted to present myself to him. I unhooked my bra.

Arthur didn't move or say anything. I stepped out of my jeans and padded closer to him, standing in the pale margin of light. His eyes were closed—I mean, fiercely closed—and he was shamming sleep. I stood there for over five minutes but he wouldn't open them. Then I stepped back, extinguished the bulb, picked up my jeans by their belt loops, my bra, my blouse, and fled.

"Kim," he whispered a couple of minutes later, standing outside my door, "may I come in? We need to talk."

I was sprawled atop the bed, my face buried in the jumbled pillows. I had not bothered to get dressed.

"Kim, please. I didn't see anything."

I knew he was lying. I wouldn't answer him.

"Listen to me. There's no reason for you to be embarrassed. Just open the door."

I was humiliated but I got up as I was and I opened the door. For a couple of seconds Arthur just stood there, looking and looking at me, all of me, his hands jammed in his pockets. Even without the lights on, I could see resistance beginning to drain right out of him. I knew then and there I'd be able to lead him back to his sofa bed, if not tonight, then tomorrow night, or the night after. And I knew that Arthur knew this too.

"Kim."

I silenced him.

"I'm going to get you a robe."

I asked him not to and rested my forehead against his shirt pocket. I could feel his fountain pen, and the metal cartridge of his drafting pencil, and beneath his leather checkbook, the wild thudding of his heart. I lifted up my face and kissed him. He did not move away. Once, when I opened my eyes, I could see that his eyes were closed.

"Kim," he murmured after a while, finally resting his chin on the top of my head. "Kim, please, you know this is impossible. You know we can't, I can't." But he didn't sound convincing.

I was beginning to shiver from the air-conditioning so he put his arms around me, his hands on the wings of my back, his fingertips gracing my spine.

My mother must have heard something because a moment later we heard her cork-soled clogs cross the living room, then clop through the foyer. At the bottom of the staircase she tentatively called our names.

"I've got to go," Arthur whispered.

I shook my head.

"Kim—"

My mother was starting up the steps, asking if anyone else was up.

I pressed my face against his chest again.

"Kim, please."

He started to turn around, stopped himself, and despite my mother's advancing footsteps, tenderly cupped my head in his hands and kissed me on the brow. Then he hurried down the staircase, meeting her halfway. My mother seemed so relieved to see him. She said she couldn't sleep either, what with the takeoff party and all. She knew it was the middle of the night, that he was probably going bonkers hearing about her airplane all the time, but she just needed his ear for a couple of minutes—he was always so objective. She had some new ideas. Well, maybe not exactly new ones but slight variations on—

I closed my door, flopped down on the quilt, and fell asleep to the buzz of my mother's plans.

Then I sat up, cold and disoriented. Shadows of clouds were sliding across the window blinds. It was 5:53 in the morning. I wrapped myself up in the quilt and headed toward the staircase. The sun hadn't reached the living room yet so everything was bathed in a leaden blue haze. I saw my mother, through the spokes of the banister, reposed on the davenport, her eyes closed, her arm draped over the cushions. Next to her hand were balls of notebook paper, and Arthur's gold fountain pen. I started down the dark steps. On the first landing, sitting with his knees drawn up, his head resting against the wallpaper, was Arthur. He didn't see me. He looked exhausted. I sensed that he didn't want any company right now. His shirt, the shadows under his eyes, even his wedding band, were cast in the cold light of the morning. I quietly retreated upstairs, curled up under the quilt, and fell into a deep and troubled sleep.

Next thing I knew it was high noon and my mother was revving up our convertible. Slipping into her robe, I hurried downstairs but by the time I got there she was already out of the driveway, speeding away. A note was propped on the coffee table:

> You looked so peaceful sleeping, darling, I didn't dare wake you. Arthur's already at the hotel, setting up posters. I wanted to wait for any last-minute queries! Will you man the phone for me? I'll call as soon as we land!! Wish me good luck! Bon voyage! Mom.

There were seven sentences and five exclamation points. No phone number where I could reach her. I crumpled up the note and chucked it into the wastebasket. I was furious she hadn't woken me. I sat down at her desk. The drawers were crammed with scraps of paper, scribbled names without phone numbers, scrawled phone numbers without names. One drawer had a legal pad covered with her doodles—a zillion profiles of the same woman's face: Kewpie doll lashes, heart-shaped lips. I closed my eyes for a moment and tried to relax but all I could see was my mother leading a flock of these identical women across a desert, away from the pyramids, insisting an airplane was coming to rescue them. After a while I must have dozed off again because the ladies vanished. And the desert turned black. And I couldn't really see or hear anything except a constant wind and my mother's voice.

"Here," she called in my dream, "over here. Hello, hello. Is anyone out there?"

Chapter Six

Three hours later the telephone rang.

"Your mother's flying the airplane. I'm the only passenger."

"Are you okay, Arthur?"

"Well, according to your mother, if nobody shows up soon, my promotion's come through. She's going to make me co-pilot. I think you should get here quick, Kim, while she's still manic."

I rubbed the sleep out of my eyes with the hem of her robe. I asked him why he hadn't said goodbye to me this morning. Was he angry with me about last night?

"Kim, you're hardly the one I'm upset with. Can we talk about last night later? This is very important. Just listen to me. I've given your mother something. She's terribly distracted and upset right now. Make sure she doesn't lose it."

I didn't know what he was talking about. I told him I just wanted him to get her out of there and come home.

"It's not possible. Your mother's locked herself in the

bathroom with the house phone and is trying to convince the bellhops from room service to get on board."

Then I suggested he just leave her there. Bail out, as my mother would say.

"Kim, please, your mother needs you. There's a bus schedule in the cutlery drawer. There should be some change in there as well. If not, I always keep a bit of cash in my desk near the right-hand—"

I said I already knew where it was. I wanted to talk about last night. Was he mad at me?

"Oh my God, Kim, no."

He wasn't just saying that?

"I am not just saying that."

"You swear?"

"Kimberly, I swear. If last night was anyone's fault, it was my own. I should have seen what was coming and stopped it before it was too late."

I wanted to know what he meant by too late.

"Nothing," he said quietly. "Nothing, honey."

He'd never called me honey before. "And you'll be there when I get there?" I asked. Something about the stifled tone of his voice frightened me.

"Just hurry, honey. And remember to take very, very good care of yourself, and of your mother."

I said I was sick of taking care of my mother. She was always coming between—

"Kim, please, I think she's about to crash."

"I doubt it," I said, cradling the receiver, "because I'm going to kill her first."

When a person is murdered, according to the tabloid, they are greeted in the next world not by their deceased loved ones but by dead acquaintances who, while they were alive, had haunted the periphery of their days—a maid, the mailman, a bellboy. Since our chemical makeup is virtually the same as sea water, I pictured these spectral hosts greeting my mother (after I strangled her) as watery silhouettes, transparent as tide pools through which she might see, for the first time in her life, other people's souls churning. Newly dead and always anxious to make friends, my mother would reach out to embrace them but her still-warm body would make it impossible; the heat from her greedy fingers would cause them to evaporate before her eyes.

I scooped the change out of Arthur's cutlery drawer and rode the bus to the Holiday Inn.

"I'm looking for a party registered as Flights Unlimited. Do you have a suite number?" I asked the hotel clerk.

"I'm afraid your party's taken off."

For one insane moment I thought Mom had succeeded.

"The woman's disappeared without paying, she left the room a sty, and two of our towels are missing."

"She didn't say where she was going?"

"Hardly."

"Was there a tall gentleman with her?"

"I don't recall."

"May I take a look at the suite?"

"Not without paying the lady's bill."

I trod across the lobby, slipped behind a plastic palm and doubled back, riding the service elevator up to the top floor. A maid was trundling a linen cart down the paisley hall. I blocked her passage for a sec, asking if she knew where Flights Unlimited was meeting.

Scrutinizing my crumpled T-shirt, frayed jeans, thonged feet, she reluctantly pointed to the last door.

"Hey, thanks," I said, reeling around.

She began wheeling the cart in the wake of my flip-flops. Actually, she confessed, she herself was considering buying a ticket. Did I know anything about the lady who ran it?

I reached for the doorknob, rattling its lock. "Could you open it?" I asked.

"I'm sorry," she said.

"Please."

"It's against our policy," she announced, nervously eyeing the empty corridor. Then, lowering her voice, she asked, was I here to reserve a seat? She'd overheard some of the bellhops discussing the lady's last-minute propositions (evidently, at the end, Mom was giving away discounts).

I said I not only knew the lady pilot, we were like this, and held up my right hand, wrapping two fingers around each other, squeezing the lifeblood out of the one that symbolized Mom. I swore that if she'd just unlock the door for me, I'd get her a deal on that airplane, whenever it took off, wherever it touched down.

She mentioned she also had a friend working in room service.

"Trust me," I said. "On this particular flight, there will be window seats for all."

She finally unlocked the door.

The king-size bed was strewn with potato chips. A couple of posters were Scotch-taped above the TV. Near the smoked-glass windows lay dozens of unused Styrofoam coffee cups and a slew of my mother's handbills. I opened the bathroom door. Floating in the porcelain toilet bowl were the remnants of my mother's flight plans, ripped up, sodden, their inky equations dissolving. I sat down on the rim of the tub and flushed them away. Something about the blue water and the whirling scraps of her loopy handwriting rushing into the vortex made me feel unbearably sad: she wasn't just eccentric or odd or unwanted, she was really nuts.

I stepped out onto the balcony to see if I could find her. A raindrop splashed on my thongs. Across the parking lot, she was warming up our blue convertible. I dashed down the six flights of stairs and breathlessly rushed out.

My mother was squeezed between two empty Cadillacs but her normally envious gaze was not directed at their pink, lacquered wings, or even at their golden grilles: it hung instead over the void of a vacant parking spot. A dry silhouette of the former car was being erased by pellets of rain. And she looked despondent.

"Roll down the window and give me the keys," I said.

She rolled down the window. "If you touch me, I'll die."

I touched her anyway. I gently wrapped my hand around the base of her neck. "You're not dead yet, Mom. Where's Arthur?"

She pointed to the empty parking spot. "Something horrible's happened."

"I already know."

"Are you going to kill me?"

"Yes."

"It's not my fault. According to my calculations, Arthur should have landed a rich man. How are you going to kill me?"

"I'm toying with the idea of strangulation."

"I guess I'll have to take off my earrings for that."

"Not if you don't struggle, Mom. If you don't struggle, I'm sure you can die with your drop earrings on."

I climbed in beside her and took the controls.

"Where are we going?" she asked.

"To find Arthur."

I veered into traffic and we sped through the wet, moonless night. At a filling station, I left her idling by the pumps while I phoned our house. No answer. If he was going home, he should have been there by now.

"Mom, did he say where he was going?"

"Oh, Kimmy, I don't remember. I was extremely preoccupied."

I released the emergency brake and we lurched off.

"I can't believe you did this," I said.

"You're not giving me a chance to tell my side of the story."

"What? What is your side of the story?"

She stared out the streaked passenger window. "I don't have a side yet."

I stopped at the next filling station. "Mom, I need another dime. I'm going to try his office."

She rummaged through her calfskin purse. "Sorry, Kim. All I have is a fiver and Arthur's money order."

"His what?"

"He paid me in advance for the first three rows of seats."

So that was what he meant when he said he'd given her something. I leaned my forehead against the cold steering wheel and started to cry.

"Kimmy, please don't be upset with me."

I wouldn't talk to her.

"Kimmy, I'm going to give him his money back."

I wouldn't look at her.

"Kimmy, just listen to me," she said, stroking my hair. "While I was waiting for you, I kept going over and over the whole airplane disaster and I can't see where I'm entirely to blame. Okay, I probably should have done a little more groundwork before the party. I might have gone after a classier clientele. But, Kim, the concept still strikes me as spectacular. Given the chance . . . well . . . I'd do it all over again. Of course, I'd do things differently now. First off, I'd conceive of a more exclusive airplane—say, a ten-seater private jet, or better yet, a rocket ship."

I yanked her hand off my hair. I looked at her wild-eyed. "Mom," I screamed, "even for a million bucks, what pilot in her right mind would jettison herself into outer space!"

"I would," she said softly. "I would."

She kept her wide-set eyes, glass-blue and bloodshot, fixed on me. Under her false eyelashes burned real tears.

There was no thunder, no flash of ozone-blue insight: I simply forgave her.

When we got home, the house was dark and Arthur's Packard was nowhere in sight. The garage door stood open (he never left it open) and I noticed that a curtain of rain had swept all the way to the oil slick. The front door wasn't locked. The welcome mat still held his puddled heel print within its wicker hem. Even before my mother turned on the lights, I knew everything was wrong. Two letters sat waiting for us on the mantel.

My mother opened hers:

> Dear Gloria,
> Please understand this decision has been made with great anguish. I don't want you to blame yourself in any way. You are not responsible for my leaving. I would have left in any case, rich or poor, pilot or passenger. It's simply too soon after my wife's death for me to live with anyone. I know this now.

I'm sorry to disappear on you and Kim in such a cowardly fashion, but had we spoken first, I might not have found the strength to leave. And it's best for everyone. Please, Gloria, believe me.

The money order I gave you should cover rent and expenses if you and Kim decide to stay here until she finishes school. The lease on the house is good for another year. The furniture is yours if you want it. I hope one day you'll forgive me.

Arthur

I tore open mine:

Dearest Kim,
Last night I realized I couldn't safely live with you and be responsible for what might . . .

I ripped my letter into two, four, eight, sixteen, thirty-two pieces. I didn't want to read it. I checked the den closet to see if he'd taken his clothes (he had) and the box of his working blueprints (he did). Then I sat down on the front porch to wait for him, convinced he would change his mind. After a while, my mother shambled outside and joined me. Each time a glimmer of headlights zoomed by, we'd both look up, following them to their vanishing point.

An hour or so passed. The rain turned into blowing drizzle. My mother finally talked me into going inside.

We slumped onto his sofa. She unfolded her letter again and slowly reread it. I tried to reassemble the puzzle pieces of mine but it was hopeless. Then I remembered his cigar box of old photographs and assured myself that if he hadn't taken them . . . I dashed upstairs. The drawer was empty. I flopped down on his sofa bed, buried my face in the top sheet and took in a deep whiff of him. Suddenly I recalled

other things he might have left that would prove he was
coming back, like the Polaroid snaps of his wife. I yanked
open the bureau drawer. He hadn't taken them. Nor had
he taken his hankies. I checked the bathroom medicine
cabinet: his striped toothbrush was still there, as were his
double-edged razor and his antihistamine pills. I tore open
the bedroom closet to see if he'd left his favorite slippers.
They were sitting amid the dust balls with the flattened
shapes of his feet embedded in their lambskin soles. I
grabbed them and headed downstairs to show my mother
but she'd fallen asleep on the sofa, her cheek crushed against
the bolster. I placed his slippers side by side on the rug,
slumped down beside her and, totally exhausted, dozed off
for a sec.

Then Arthur's headlamps broke through the blinds and
the whole house lit up. I popped open my eyes. But the
beam was coming from the antechamber of my dream, and
the real room was dark and still and empty, save for the
silhouette of my mother and the sound of her shallow snoring.

Arthur didn't return that night, or the next day, or the
day after that. I phoned his office, his late wife's sister, a
couple of engineers he sometimes had drinks with, even the
doctor who'd attended my mother after the accident, but no
one would say where he was. Their voices sounded curt and
cold. You could tell they thought that Arthur had done the
right thing by fleeing us, that he'd been nuts to take us in
to begin with. And all I remember about the rest of that
week was the static view from the porch where I spent
hours waiting for him—the carved back of my mother's Tiki,
the neighbor's blue ice plant, the tin garbage pails, the curb

and its stenciled addresses—all changing from lead dawn to sunstruck noon to dusk to endless night.

I was devastated.

Los Angeles does have seasons. After August's still heat and flash storms come September's searing winds. It took my mother and me almost until the end of the Santa Anas to admit to ourselves that he wasn't coming back.

We were sitting on the front lawn. Fire season had begun. Across the valley, flames were already blackening the spine of a mountain where the more exclusive homes sat in tiers. From time to time a whole ridge would flare up. The sun was a cindery disk. Our own street looked as if it might buckle in the heat. Really, there was no point in our staying here any longer.

I wanted to know what we were going to do.

"I don't know," my mother sighed. In some ways, she was more lost without Arthur than I was. She squinted up at the sky, then down at the pebble-strewn driveway. "I can still see the old skid marks from our collision."

I glanced with smarting eyes at the black tire treads.

"You really were in love with him, weren't you, Kimmy?"

I shrugged.

"I guessed as much. Just call it mother's intuition." She tucked a coil of my hair behind my ear. "Maybe he'll still come back?"

I shook my head.

"I don't think so either. I'm so sorry, Kim."

I rubbed my eyes with the heel of my hand. She propped herself up on her elbows.

"If you want, we could stick around here until you finish school."

I said I didn't think I could handle living in his house without him.

She squinted back at the porch, the mailbox, his garage. "I don't think I'm up for it myself," she sighed. Then she stood up, her red scarf whipping back and forth. "I guess we could go on the road again."

"I don't want to go on the road again."

"How about moving to the high desert?"

"I don't want to move to the high desert."

"You sure? My Nevada customers probably haven't touched a woman in six months. They must be frothing by now. I'll bet we could make our fortune there."

I shook my head again, but with the wind and the dust and the smoke and her illusions, she just didn't see me.

"Empires crumble and from their ashes new empires rise. Didn't Patricia Neal make a big comeback after her stroke? I only had a concussion, Kim."

"Mom, sit down and listen to me."

She sat down.

"I'll stick it out with you this year until I finish high school but after that, you're on your own. I want to go to college."

"Okay, I'll live in the vicinity of your campus. Those fraternity boys are probably oozing pheromones all on their own. How about this for a catchy campus slogan: 'Gloria's Aphrodisiac Perfume: *We tap into your sap.*' "

"Mom, you're not hearing me."

"Okay, I know it's not right yet but I'm veering toward a marketing concept that will appeal to the sophomoric crowd. I feel our customers will fall into the C minus category."

I looked down at the grass, then out at the haze, past the fires and the smoke, to where distance itself appeared to collapse in its own heat.

"Mom, you can't come with me," I said.

Chapter Seven

The black-and-white scenes of college have no place in my story beside the Technicolor, larger-than-life world of my mother. During those four lonely years of study, when every crack in reality was immediately corked by a teacher's rational explanation, her letters, scribbled on the back of coffee shop napkins and postcards, became more important to me than biology or physics, time, space, or relativity.

How could the list of scientists I jotted down and repeated to myself at night, a litany of genius I'd once hoped to emulate—Galileo, Newton, Einstein—compare with the postcard list my mother mailed me from Hollywood, California?

Dear Kim,

I just took a meeting with Ernest Borgnine's wife's hairdresser. There are definitely film possibilities in my life story. Perhaps something dreamed up by Walt Disney. Opening shot: Wanted Poster. Slowly the composite police sketch grows more and more animated until it dissolves into the actress who plays me. Who? Who? Who?

A list of actresses, alphabetized in schoolgirl fashion, filled the rest of the postcard:

> Andrews, Julie
> Ball, Lucille
> Bancroft, Anne
> Coca, Imogene (only as last resort)
> Dickinson, Angie
> Jones, Jennifer
> MacLaine, Shirley
> Margret, Ann
> Pleshette, Suzanne
> Reed, Donna
> Saint, Eva Marie
> Seberg, Jean
> Wood, Natalie
> Young, Loretta

If the origin of our species is a mystery, as my anthropology professor said, and each of our genes carries a stratagem of animal traits, wasn't my mother on the frontier of science when she wrote:

> I just got slapped with another fine by the Postmaster General. I don't think he's totally human, Kim.

And how could I possibly concentrate on studying for my midterm examinations when her multiple-choice letter arrived?

Here's the problem. One of the local networks is bringing back a new version of *What's My Line?* (remember the old game show where people with weird professions tried to outsmart a panel of witty celebrities?). I've talked to a number of people in the business and they all believe I would make an ideal contestant (think of the free advertising! What a perfect climax for the movie version of my life story!). I'm filling out the application form right now. My question is: How should I bill myself?

a. Should I try to shock the producers with my aphrodisiac perfumes?

b. Do I try to promote some of my less risqué products like my new weight loss machine that hooks up to a vacuum cleaner?

c. Do I just mention all my products and let them decide?

d. None of the above.

Please write back as soon as you can. It's all I can think about.

I closed my textbooks. I stretched out on my dorm room cot. "Mom," I wrote her back, "I believe answer a's your best bet."

Over the course of our correspondence, I received letters on napkins from Dolly's, Duke's, Bob's Big Boy, Howard Johnson's, not to mention truck stops: The Pit, Bull and Beer, Gracie's. Technicolor postcards, dog-eared and torn, flew in from Needles, California (a giant needle piercing the desert), Las Vegas, Nevada (Liberace at his glass piano), the Queen Mary Ocean Liner, Long Beach (the *Queen Mary* ocean liner), and, of course, Hollywood, California (Gloria Swanson donning a pair of winged sunglasses just like my mom's).

Invariably all her schemes fizzled out and evaporated: her perfume empire never got off the ground again, her life story proved unmarketable, the *New What's My Line?* producers kept putting her off, and even she wasn't sure how to market and sell the weight loss machine that hooked up to a vacuum cleaner. From time to time I'd get collect calls from Tucson, Bullhead City, Thousand Palms, or San Bernardino. "Do you remember . . . ?" my mother inevitably began.

"Do you remember my Hawaiian Tiki, Kim?"

"It's difficult to forget, Mom."

"Well, the other day, even though it was completely out of my way, I drove by the old homestead."

My breath caught.

"A new family's moved in. A Sears, Roebuck mom and dad, complete with freckled kids. I asked them if Arthur left a forwarding address."

Pause. Phone static. Heartbeat.

"I'm sorry, Kim, he hadn't. Are you okay?"

"Not really."

My mother and I were both silent for a moment. I could hear the dull drumming of her chewed fingernails against the glass phone booth.

"Anyway, do you want to hear about my Tiki?" she finally asked.

"Mom, I want to hear about your Tiki more than anything else in the world right now." I wasn't lying.

"Well, Mr. Sears, Roebuck and son were trying to dig it out of the front lawn with pitchforks and shovels. They're probably roasting it in the fireplace right now, where Arthur's hickory logs used to be. Do you think he ever thinks about us?"

"Mom, we forced him to flee his own house. I'm sure he thinks about us all the time."

Then I hung up, my forehead slumped against the wall phone. Whatever ability I had left to study vanished. I thought my love for Arthur would have faded by now, but it hadn't. That evening I stretched out on my dorm room cot and I fixed my gaze on the ceiling and I tried to will my love away, to steel my heart against him. Whenever a memory of him arose—his pipe in an ashtray, the smell of his cologne, his shower thongs on the bathroom tiles—I'd scour it for its insignificance. But since my love was lodged not so much in my heart now as in my memories, without being able to stop myself I'd see his feet fill the shower thongs, or smell his skin beneath his cologne, or watch the embers of his pipe flare up from his breath. And I'd be beside myself with longing again.

That night I didn't sleep. I lay curled on my cot, staring at my mother's postcards, my muddled and disorganized class notes, a photo I'd kept of Arthur. By morning I'd decided to drop out of school for a while.

I packed my duffel bag and hitchhiked down the West Coast. I slept in geodesic domes, in Volkswagen vans, once under a crooked cypress in a soupy fog with the black Pacific lapping near my ears. I attended be-ins and hung out on the denimed fringes of love-ins, my hands jammed in my pockets, looking on. I passed the bong around with strangers, and swilled wine from goatskin pouches as Greek peasants do. I dropped hallucinogens and witnessed the world as I imagined my mother did—a place where the seams between dimensions leak light and possibilities. I slept with men to see if I could counteract my love for Arthur and taught myself a mindless, if temporary, bliss. One had Arthur's ears, another his wrists. I took day jobs—strawberry picker, artichoke sorter, door-to-door salesgal. And whenever I had a couple of bucks, I'd mail out a slew of letters to all my mother's PO boxes, knowing one would reach her. One evening we rendezvoused at a truck stop near Fresno and the next dawn, walking past a store window, I glimpsed myself for what I'd become—an itinerant like my mother, but without her mad dreams.

I caught the next Greyhound bus back to Berkeley. I reenrolled in school. I crammed for my classes. When one of her postcards flew in, I didn't let myself get involved in her harebrained schemes. I made progress—A's in physics, B's in astronomy. I combed the want ads. I found a job as a tour guide in the children's wing of the Oakland Planetarium, part-time now, full-time after graduation. I even began pricing apartments in the cheaper suburbs—furnished or unfurnished, I didn't care which, as long as the place had a stable lease.

And the week before I finally graduated, my mother mailed her last postcard:

> Why not invest in your future, Kim, and become my silent partner in a metal detector? Do you have any of your student loan left?

I wired her the last of my dwindling funds. Then I closed my eyes and envisioned this:

My mother is standing on a sand dune. She is wearing her winged sunglasses, maroon slacks, and yellow halter top. The wind is beginning to kick up and grains of quartz, amethyst, basalt, and rose are blowing across her sandaled feet, erasing her footprints, the mad, concentric path she has taken to reach this dune, on this beach, at this hour. The light has started to diminish. The sky is orange, the sea is tar green, with broken refractions of the sunset drifting back and forth, back and forth in the troughs of sluggish waves. My mother is combing the beach with her metal detector. She is using a system for search and recovery unlike any system I've read about in school. She is not thorough, or methodical, there is no logic whatsoever in her wanderings. No, my mother is wildly swinging her metal detector up and down, up and down the dunes, her sandals clopping, her winged sunglasses slipping down the bridge of her nose, madly scanning the sand for lost riches. She keeps her eyes fixed solely on the metal gauge, hoping, hoping the needle will go nuts and shoot off the scales. On her sunburned shoulder hangs a plastic grocery bag wherein lie all the treasures she's exhumed so far: four dimes, eight nickels, three quarters, a Timex watch, an identification bracelet with *Rick loves Lori* engraved on it, three charms— a gold heart, a gold horse, a gold tennis racket—one nail clipper, and six slugs. It is almost nighttime but my mother doesn't want to go home. The sand, sea and air are now the same color, a mixture of lilac and phosphorescent green. It is really too dark for her to see anything and so, reluctantly, she swings her metal detector up over her shoulder.

But this is what I hope: that although she never knew it, the needle on her metal gauge went nuts, that buried under one of the sand dunes is a sunken silver-gray Mercedes Benz with red interior, that even though she'll never drive it, she did stumble upon her finest hour. Please understand, the silver-gray Mercedes Benz with red interior is only a shell, the spirit made flesh, an earthly embodiment of something far more spiritual and glorious to my mother. In one miraculous instant, her lifetime of hope and confusion, dream and disenchantment will have all become a zany anecdote to be told over aperitifs and hors d'oeuvres.

Then my mother turns to go home and the lapping water rushes over her cold toes.

Part Two

Weightlessness

Chapter Eight

I was again pulling into a windy trailer park, this time in the flood-scarred canyons outside of Searchlight, Nevada, where my mother was temporarily stranded. She'd blown a piston two weeks before, en route to Hollywood (after innumerable disappointments, she'd finally been accepted as a contestant on *The New What's My Line?*). She'd pleaded with me to take a week off work to be her cheering section and chauffeur. I was more than a little nervous: my own life (first apartment, six-month-old job) was still so fragile and untested that one strong tug from my mother's world might easily unravel it.

I braked at the top of the hill. I had to keep swallowing because of the high altitude, and I had to keep rubbing my eyes because, from the moment my tires had swung into the park, everything was blowing and blurred with double-take familiarity—clotheslines, screen doors, tumbleweeds (the same kind of thorn-and-thistle bushes I'd scratched my six-year-old knees on)—and then, blowing across my highbeams, a lawn chair somersaulted toward me in the dust.

It was almost dark but I could still make out our trailer a couple of Airstreams away, bucking in the wind, and I could see the back of my mother's Aztec-stripe popover housecoat slapping against her thighs as she stood on the front steps, up on her tiptoes, surveying the wrong road in the wrong direction for me.

I didn't honk or anything, I just wanted to sit there for a while behind the tinted windshield and watch her. The way she toed the ground in her impatience, the way her thin hair whipped back and forth, the way the world of my childhood fluttered and heaved before me.

And I remember saying aloud to myself: "You don't have to go through with this. Just turn around. She won't even know you've been here. Phone later with some excuse. An important breakthrough . . . No, a miraculous scientific discovery . . . No, a miraculous scientific discovery that could lead to a big promotion (the less plausible, the more she'll believe it) was happening at the planetarium on, say, Monday, and you had to be there. Just make sure that if she doesn't win the jackpot, you wire her money from time to time."

Then I was out of the car and in her arms.

My mother and I had not seen each other in almost two years (since the day we'd rendezvoused at a truck stop during our months of parallel drifting). I sat down on the coconut chair. She sank into the swayback sofa, then reeled around and piled the bolsters so she could sit bolt upright to study me in my new adult countenance: my first crow's feet, my newly veined wrists, the nervous habit I'd acquired of raking my hand through my hair.

"Hey," she said.

"Hey," I said.

I raked my hand through my hair.

She fingered the hem of her housecoat and just looked and looked at me. I knew she was grappling with a way to ask me about my life, but everything she could think of—apartment leases and car payments, quasars and gamma rays—was just outside the orbit of her knowledge.

"Well," she said, slapping her thighs.

"Well," I said, shrugging.

Then she leaned over (I drew in a deep whiff of her—Lillies of the Valley: my mother never wore her own perfumes) and she tenderly kissed my brow.

"Would you like to see all the changes I made in the trailer, kid?"

"You bet."

"You're not just saying that, Kim. I mean, you're really interested?"

"Of course."

"Because, you know"—she made a small sweeping gesture with her right hand: the same gesture I use when giving my tour on the Milky Way—"all this is going to be yours someday."

She showed me some brick contact paper she'd slapped up over the range, and a new paper towel rack, and a burl-wood coffee table she'd picked up for a song.

"And I stocked the refrigerator with all your favorite foods. I even put the Mars bars in the freezer, just like you like them, Kimmy." She opened the freezer door and a waft of tepid air floated out. "Something's happened to the thermostat, though, so the caramel's not really frozen yet. I was hoping you'd take a look at it later."

I said I would.

"Also, the water in the kitchen sink isn't going down the drain properly and . . . really, Kim"—she sank back onto the sofa, folding one leg under her—"I don't know why I'm so fond of this dump."

A caravan of trucks thundered by. The trailers adjacent to the highway rocked, headlights washing over them. For a moment they glowed against the cavernous night sky like aluminum foil logs.

"Do you know what the people in those trailers wish for?"

I said I didn't know.

"Getting my spot in the park, that's all."

Then she led me into my old bedroom—a tubular wedge at the front of the trailer with a tiny louvered window.

"I just changed the sheets yesterday. I've been using the place as a storeroom for my perfumes. I'm not like one of those mothers who, after their kids leave home, turn their bedrooms into a shrine or anything."

I flopped down on my old cot and bounced a couple of times. "It still has some spring."

"I guess it's good for a couple more years."

Stretching out, I rested my head on my old pillow, the scent and yield of which were as familiar to me as breathing.

"You're tired, huh?" she asked.

"I've been driving since dawn."

"You know we have to get an early start tomorrow. It's a six-hour trek to Hollywood and I'll need some time to get my beauty sleep before my big debut on Monday. I wouldn't want the *What's My Line?* panel to guess I'm a professional zombie."

I nodded.

"We'll catch up on all your latest adventures mañana."

"Mom, I understand."

"Well, you know where everything is. I mean, aside from the brick contact paper et al., I haven't done any major renovations."

Then she started out the door, stopped, and pivoted on her sandal-shod foot. "Kimmy, do you still like a glass of water next to your bed?"

I said I did. I said I was touched she remembered.

And she returned with a paper cup of water.

But later that evening, well past midnight, she came in one more time. My light was off but I was awake, racked with misgivings. I didn't want to go to Hollywood tomorrow. I didn't want to be in this trailer, back in her world, with the perpetual lure of the highway outside, the musk of her dreams all around, the aluminum walls closing in.

I feigned sleep, cracking open one eye to watch her.

She was wearing a pair of eyeglasses I'd never seen on her before (not sequined or winged, but big and round and pink and bifocaled) and she just stood there, at the foot of my bed, with her temple resting against the wall, looking and looking at me.

By sunup, we were on the road again, barreling down Interstate 15. My mother was at the wheel of my Volkswagen, her freshly dyed blond hair pinned up for her big debut and tucked neatly under a rajah turban so that it wouldn't "whip into a fur ball." I was in the passenger seat, my nose slathered with white zinc, reading one of our old road maps. And for every landmark that whizzed past—The Gold Strike, a casino standing in the shadow of the Nevada State Penitentiary; Kactus Kate's flamingo-pink sign LAST LOOSE SLOTS BEFORE CALIFORNIA; the Flying A gasoline station in Death Valley; the eucalyptus windbreaks with their silver-and-taupe leaves—my mother would say, "Do you remember that one, Kim?" And I wasn't sure if I did remember, or even wanted to: the strangest images were coming back to me—our odometer at 41,206 miles; my mother's foot, ten years younger, the toenails painted coral red, flooring the accelerator, a hurly-burly of years and speed, mirages and dead ends, racing across the tropical-green lenses of her winged sunglasses. And then we were slowing down, circling the giant four-leaf clover of the Harbor and Hollywood Freeway interchange and gliding down the ramp at Vine where my mother, all bronzed and gritty from the wind, pulled into a tiny stucco motel off Hollywood Boulevard and said, "Oh, come on, Kimmy, you must remember the first time I took you to Hollywood and we stayed here?"

And I remembered: She had reserved us a "special" second-story, north-facing room in this particular motel because, when she lifted me up to the aluminum casement window over the bathtub and gently pressed my five-year-old cheek against the cold glass, I could just make out the HO in the HOLLYWOOD sign.

We unpacked, carefully hanging up my mother's debut suit for tomorrow. Then, despite our exhaustion, she insisted on taking me out on the town, to one of her old haunts, Johnnie's Steak House, a sort of hoi polloi version of Musso and Frank's, the old movie star hangout.

"Unfortunately," my mother explained a couple of minutes later, as we were sliding into one of Johnnie's red booths, "this place tends to attract the starlets and starmen after they've descended."

We ordered a couple of Johnnie's Sunday night specials.

"Could you rehearse with me, Kim?" she asked as soon as the waitress left. "At least until the main course arrives."

"Mom, I never saw the show."

"It's exactly like twenty questions. Just ask me if I perform a service."

"Okay. Do you perform a service?"

"No. Ask me if I sell a product."

"Do you sell a product?"

"Yes! Okay, ask me something else."

"Is your product legal to send through the United States mail?"

"Really, Kim, this is very important to me."

"I'm sorry. Is your product used by both men and women?"

"No."

"Men?"

"Yes."

"Is your product bigger than a breadbox?"

"No."

"Smaller than"—I looked around for inspiration—"a ketchup bottle?"

"Yes."

"Is your product utilitarian?"

Long pause while my mother toyed with the straw in her Coca-Cola.

"Mom?"

"I don't know."

"Is it something men need?"

Suddenly my mother let go of her straw and gulped down the mouthful of soda pop she had just taken and put down her bubbly glass.

"Don't turn around, Kim," she said in a soft voice, "but directly behind you is someone who was somebody a couple of years ago."

She quietly snapped open her purse and handed me her compact mirror.

I positioned it in such a way as to reflect as many of Johnnie's patrons as I could fit into its round, smudged surface. Remember, in the intervening years, I'd lost my mother's ability to retouch the world and defuse its sharp edges and all I could make out in the tiny glass were a couple of elderly men in loud check suits and polo shirts, sitting alone in red booths, cutting up what appeared to be Salisbury steak, and suddenly I wanted to cry.

"Enough of that stargazing, Kim," my mother said. "Ask me if my product is—"

"Mom, is your product something men can taste? Touch? Inhale? Hold? Feel? Want? Desire?"

That night, as my mother slept soundly (with two alarm clocks running beside her), I sat on the edge of our bed, my legs drawn up, my chin on my knees. It wasn't cold but I was shivering. A palm frond scratched against the air conditioner grille. The violet shaft of a searchlight, on the other side of the Hollywood hills, swept around the night sky. Over my mother's pillow hung a painting of a sunset with far-reaching rays and four metal screws pierced through its frame to thwart theft.

I rested my head against the bed board and watched her for a while—curled up under the sheets, breathing raggedly, absolutely oblivious to this world. Her mouth was open in dreamer's awe, probably following some mad plot. I wandered into the bathroom and shut the door. I just needed to be alone for a moment before her alarms went off and I was back in her world.

I sat down on the rim of the tub and stared out the casement window. I could see the pink minarets of the Egyptian Theater, the on ramp that led to the freeway that led to Oakland and my apartment, the neon satellite above Astro-Burger, and farther up, lit by a sepia spotlight and looking truly grand on the crest of the hills, the *H* and the *O* of the HOLLYWOOD sign. The rest of the letters were cut off by a concrete retaining wall.

"*Today's my* big debut, kid. How do I look?"

She was already dressed, standing above me, her hair teased into a cumulus effect, a kiss curl plastered on her furrowed brow. The stark light of the morning burned through the half-open blinds. She looked old.

"Terrific," I said.

"Really, Kim, don't lie. Besides, the worse I look, the better my chances are for stumping the panel." She chucked me my clothes and approached the mirror to take one last gander at herself: first full-face, then profile. "I mean, who in their right mind is going to guess that this decrepit old thing has sold aphrodisiacs for the past twenty years."

"You're going to be loved by millions," I said.

"Hey, it's only a syndicated rehash, Kim. What kind of nut watches game shows on local TV?"

On the boulevard, hurrying down the gold-flecked sidewalk that led to the television studios, my mother stopped for a moment to gaze down at the stars. "Do you know what I really wish," she admitted.

I hadn't the slightest idea.

"I really wish I'd gotten on *What's My Line?* during its heyday, with John Daly and the gang. That had class, kid. Perhaps Bennett Cerf would have asked me to write my autobiography. And I could have exchanged witticisms with Dorothy Kilgallen. I might have become a cult figure of sorts. A real Lucille Ball. One that didn't have a Ricky to save her. I am so nervous, Kim," she sighed, plodding on. "I haven't told you this, but I've been practicing my signature, just like a schoolgirl, for that moment when the host says, 'Will our contestant sign in please.' "

We were greeted at the studio doors by a poker-faced, teenage usherette, who handed my mother the following rules:

> Welcome to *The New What's My Line?* Contestants are forbidden to talk with anyone before airtime; that includes other contestants, personal guests, and/or members of the audience. In addition, contestants may not wave, point, or in any fashion whatsoever signal or receive signals from members of the audience. If a contestant has to use the lavatory, an usher or an usherette must be present. We wish you all the luck in the world.

Then she was led away.

I took a front-row seat in the audience, watching the bustle of electricians and gaffers. For a moment I caught a glimpse of her, slouched against a Coke machine in the wings. And I think she saw me too, but under the scrutiny of her teenage duenna, she just looked at me without a flicker of recognition on her face. Then a buzzer blared, and the technicians retreated, and a microphone was rolled onto the stage. The director counted off the seconds—four, three, two, one—and Bill Blair, the host, fabulously tanned, the Brylcreemed part in his steel-gray hair a work of geometry, tripped down a couple of glitter-strewn steps in time to his theme song and welcomed us all to *The New What's My Line?*

The audience hooted and thumped.

Then everyone grew quiet as Bill approached the microphone. "Will our first contestant sign in pleeeeeease," he said.

Dressed in her new beige tweed skirt and caramel blazer, with a white satin blouse, white fishnet stockings, and black pumps, my mother clicked onto the soundstage.

An arm emerged from the wings holding up an APPLAUSE sign and everyone clapped.

My mother flashed a toothy smile at all three wheeling cameras, then faced the blackboard, took a deep breath, and meticulously signed her name, looping her *l*'s and dotting her *i*'s, and even blushing charmingly when the chalk accidentally squeaked.

Bill came over and shook her hand.

"Welcome to *The New What's My Line?*" he said.

My mother slid into the contestant's chair.

"Gloria, why don't you tell us a little something about yourself."

"I'm from Southern California, Bill, and thereabouts."

"And do you have any hobbies, Gloria?"

My mother was taken aback for a second. She blinked into the lights. "I travel," she said.

"I hope that's not a clue."

"It's not, Bill."

"And is there anyone you want to say hello to today?"

"I'd like to say hi to my daughter, Kim, who's visiting me from the Bay Area. She's in the audience."

"Well, Gloria, are you ready to stump the panel?"

"I am, Bill."

"But first . . ."

A huge door revolved and Tanya Latour, a comely redhead enveloped in a skintight, sequined gown sauntered out to show my mother all the prizes she could win. Tanya demonstrated the consolation prize, a massage recliner, by reposing, in a shimmering blur, on its crushed velvet cushions. Tanya touched, with a blood-red nail, the silver wing of a cardboard airplane that would jet my mother off to Lake Tahoe. And finally she pulled out, from God knows where (there were no pockets on her gown), the grand prize, a check for two thousand bucks.

Bill Blair grinned and my mother, with stoic dignity, faced her panel—two sitcom comedians and the handsome hawklike star of a soap.

"Are you ready, Gloria?" Bill asked.

My mother officiously cleared her throat. The chintz curtain behind her, catching every glint of light, looked like a glass pitcher shattering on the floor. "I am, Bill," she said and the panel began firing questions at her.

"Gloria, do you perform an act?"

"No."

"Do you provide a service?"

"No."

"Do you sell a product?"

"Yes."

"Is your product something you use by yourself?"

"Bill, do I have to answer strictly yes or no?"

"That's right, Gloria."

"I guess I'll have to answer yes, sometimes."

"Is your product used by both men and women?"

"No."

"Men?"

"Yes."

"Is your product something men might use with their kids?"

"No."

"In a group?"

"Of what?"

"Other men?"

"Yes. Why not?"

"Is it something men operate?"

"No."

"Ingest?"

"No."

"Wear?"

"Yes."

"Do they wear it at work?"

"Yes."

"At play?"

"Yes."

"For recreation?"

"Yes."

"Do they wear it below the waist?"

"No."

"Is it medicinal?"

Long pause.

"Gloria, the seconds are ticking."

"I suppose I have to say no."

"Do they wear it for pleasure?"

"Yes."

"To keep them warm?"

"Yes."

"For health?"

"Yes."

"Is it an article of clothing?"

"No."

"Jewelry?"

"No."

"Sports gear?"

"No."

The buzzer sounded. My mother had stumped the panel. She slumped momentarily in her seat, stunned, arcing her penciled brows, mouthing, "I won?" The audience clapped and clapped. Bill Blair threw up his hands and winked at the camera.

"Gloria," he boomed in a loud deep voice, "let's find out WHAT YOUR LINE IS!"

"Well, Bill," my mother said, suddenly impatient for the last throbs of applause to subside, "I sell aphrodisiac perfumes."

"Boy, oh boy, Gloria, meet me in the wings after the show."

Instructed by the LAUGH sign, the audience burst into hoots of raucous laughter. My mother fingered the hem of her skirt and smiled politely—lips curled, the cords of her powdered neck taut.

"No, really, Gloria," Bill said seriously, "tell us all about it."

"Well, Bill, have you ever heard of pheromones?" My mother didn't wait for his answer. "A bull struts past a herd and suddenly the cows go nuts. There are other steers

around. Why this guy? The answer is pheromones, a subliminal scent, the scientific proof of animal magnetism. I
work with the human equivalent, Bill, mixing one tiny drop
of the stuff into my perfumes—after all, pheromones can
overcome a two-thousand pound animal—and my customers
tell me the results are wild. No one knows exactly how it
works in human beings—I can't make any guarantees—
but, say, a gal walks into a room and she's suddenly attracted
to a man, I mean really, really floored by the guy. He hasn't
said a word. He's not even handsome—a Bogart, maybe, or
an Onassis type—but he's got it. Why? Pheromones."

"Thank you, Gloria," Bill said. Then, glancing over his
shoulder, he shot a gaga look at the audience as if to say,
"Where do we find them?"

I wanted to kill him.

But Tanya had reappeared holding up the grand prize
check. Camera one zoomed in to show a close-up of the
transfer (from Tanya's red fingernails to my mother's new
ceramic ones); camera two focused in on my mother's face
(eyebrows knitted, scrutinizing her prize); and camera three
panned out to show the whole glitter-strewn stage (my
mother wasn't jumping up and down as she'd been instructed to do, she was standing woodenly between Bill and
Tanya, waving her check above her head like a football
pennant). Then the *New What's My Line?* theme song kicked
in again and my mother was escorted off the stage, past the
hooting audience, whose wild applause, egged on by the
APPLAUSE sign, drowned out the click of her heels.

"*What is* this big deal everyone makes about success? I feel
nothing," my mother said.

We were back in our motel room. She sat slouched in the overstuffed red spring chair, her fishnetted leg hooked over the arm, her foot idly dandling. She hadn't yet changed out of her debut skirt or removed her television makeup or chosen her "motel memento"—a bar of sample soap or a face towel or a fork from room service.

"Mom," I said, "ten minutes to checkout time. You don't want to squander your winnings by having to pay an extra day in this dump, do you?"

She shrugged. I brought her a wet washcloth and helped her dab off some of that television makeup.

"Listen," I said, "we'll celebrate as soon as we get back to Searchlight. I'll drive you to Kactus Kate's. We've got to go, Mom, or we'll hit rush hour." I threw everything into the suitcases. "Do you want me to pack you some sample soap?"

"No."

"Okay. A fork? The pillowcases?" (My mother was incapable of leaving a motel room without taking something.)

"It's not necessary, Kim. I have my winnings."

She held up her game show check and stared at it, front and back, running her finger over her embossed name. Then she shook her head, and her wide-set eyes drifted away from her winnings to the yellow lampshade, then to the olive-green rug, then to the motes of dust wafting in a corner, and finally to nothing at all.

"It's astonishing," she said.

"What?" I was checking the drawers to see if we'd forgotten anything.

"The taste of victory. I don't seem to be able to savor it."

"I'm sure you will, Mom," I said, grabbing our bags and ushering her out the door. "You've been looking forward to this win for so long, you're probably just in shock."

"I don't think so," she said.

As we inched along Hollywood Boulevard in bumper-to-bumper traffic, she didn't look down at the stars or up at the Capitol Records building, her favorite landmark, designed to resemble a stack of records. Once on the highway, she didn't run me through her gauntlet of memories. She just sat quietly beside me, in the passenger seat, her wind-chapped elbow on the window gutter, her hair whipping back and forth.

"You know," she said finally, "I'm nearly fifty-two, Kim, but I believe today marks the end of my youth."

Then she cranked down her bucket seat and stretched out, staring up at the enormous dusk. To the east the sky was ultramarine shot with funnels of black mist, to the west silver-tooled clouds hung motionless in pink-and-gold space. Lightning was flashing along the horizon. The hood of my Volkswagen, with its winged ornament, was passing into darkness.

My mother glanced down at the odometer. We were exactly halfway between the trailer park and Hollywood, day and night, reality and a dream, and suddenly I had the odd sensation drivers experience after innumerable hours on a flat highway, in a landscape that never changes: we were going nowhere, we weren't moving, what had happened never took place, our tires were spinning to no avail.

I turned to my mother but she was staring out the window at the rush of sagebrush and sand, her cheek crushed against the simulated leather. In the waning light, her features looked almost invisible but I could just make out, by the pale glow of my dashboard, the Technicolor proof of her victory: a tinge of azure eyeliner, a shadow of coral rouge.

Chapter Nine

That night, when we got back to the trailer, my mother curled up on her sleeping berth and asked to be alone for a while. She claimed she wasn't up to celebrating at Kactus Kate's. I should run along if I liked, she'd even front me a roll of quarters to play the slots. Right now, what she needed was time to think.

I sat down beside her on the cushions. Her hands were folded behind her head, a band of pale moonlight crossed her throat.

"Mom," I said, "you are aware that you won today?"

She gave a deep sigh and nodded.

"That you stumped the panel? That you were"—why not exaggerate, what difference would it make?—"that you were the toast of the show?"

"I know."

"And you should be out celebrating?"

"It's not what I feel like doing, Kimmy. Oh, don't worry, I'm not depressed. I'm not experiencing any 'Is that all there is?' syndrome. Believe me, I understand the difference. This is something much more profound than that."

I went into my bedroom, closed the door, and slumped my forehead against the louvered window. I couldn't see the desert but I could hear it, its drone and howl whistling through the jamb. First thing tomorrow I'd get her piston repaired, then help her dream up some windfall scheme on which she could set her cockamamy sights, then send her on the road again so that I could return to my own life and—

I heard the front door slam. The ghost of her housecoat slipped past my window. I cupped my eye directly on the screen. My mother was heading into the desert. I grabbed my windbreaker and followed her through the trailer park, hanging back so that she wouldn't see me. She was walking along the gulch, past the Cyclone fence, up to the craggy outcrop that shielded Searchlight from desert twisters. Tumbleweeds blew by. The moon was gibbous. Enormous boulders cast skillet-flat shadows. At the top of the outcrop, she stopped for a moment to catch her breath. Then, elbows bent, she hoisted herself up onto a flat boulder. I crouched behind a rock. The air was ion-charged. Standing upright, she swayed on the top of the rock. I peeked over the black rim. Below her lay the largest expanse of nothingness I'd ever seen. Behind her, about two hundred yards down the gully, sat our Tinkertoy-size trailer park. My mother gazed out at the black void, back at the tiny trailer park, again at the shifting sands, and then again at her burning porch light—a tiny speck of brightness four hundred miles south-east of Los Angeles, two hundred miles due north of Needles.

In two days I would be leaving her. I couldn't imagine where she was going to go.

A sudden gust of wind almost lifted her off her sandaled feet and for a moment she looked weightless.

Then, setting her feet on terra firma again, she hunkered down, slid off the boulder, dusted off her housecoat, and slowly walked down the stone gully toward her glowing porch light.

"*Kimmy,*" *she* said the next morning, "I've decided to get a job."

It was six A.M. I had to pull myself up out of leaden sleep. "Mom, what are you talking about?"

"Last night it finally dawned on me—a cycle of my life is over." She sat down on the edge of my cot, drawing up her knees. "A job, Kimmy. Before I throw all my winnings away on another ridiculous scheme, I'm going to look for a real job."

"Mom, you're really serious about this?"

"Dead serious."

"You know it's going to be difficult."

"I know."

"You've never actually worked for anyone or punched a clock."

"Darling, I understand what you're driving at."

"I've got to tell you, Mom," I said, embracing her, "I think it's a terrific idea."

"Well, it's certainly an idea whose time has come."

I swung my legs over the side of the mattress and thought for a moment. "I'll bet we could find you something in sales. You're an extraordinary saleswoman. Why not? With all your experience and everything—"

"No. I don't want the heartbreak of working on a com-

mission. I want something stable. A nine-to-five. With benefits. Maybe at the post office, under an assumed name of
course. They have security. I want security. They have a
medical plan. I want a medical plan. They have a retirement
pension. I'll tell you, Kimmy, I wouldn't mind retiring. You
know, sometimes I think I've been living in a dream world.
I'll have a vision, a mirage really, like believing that a winning performance on *What's My Line?* will make all the
difference, or even my airplane idea, and for a split second
I'm sure I can make a better life for everyone, for you,
Kimmy. But what does that mean, a better life? Fame?
Lights, cameras? A big house? Not having to look at the
prices on a menu? One moment you're driving down the
road holding your little girl's hand and the next she's at the
wheel, trying to hold you together, and then you're both
gone. A better life? What does it mean?"

I stared down at the floor and tried to envision my mother
at a job interview—what was I thinking? No one would
hire her.

After breakfast she headed down to the Quonset hut grocery store to buy all the newspapers with classified sections.
She said she wanted to mull over her prospects. I watched
her from the kitchen window, trudging along the shoulder
of the highway, stopping now and then to dig a pebble out
of her cork soles, or rub the sand and glare from her eyes,
or gaze transfixed at the flash of an oil tanker truck thun-
dering into the distance. In her flapping housecoat, she
looked absurdly small and vulnerable against the enormous
landscape. I knew I couldn't leave her like this.

That afternoon I phoned the planetarium and asked for
another week off. Then I began the arduous task of trying
to distract her from looking for a real job—let's face it, there

was nothing out there for her. I took her to Kactus Kate's, hoping that the lights, bells, dice and clanging coins would jar her back to her old self. Driving home, I thought up schemes and planted them like hypnotic suggestions in her ear while she slept, mouth open, in my windy Volkswagen. Next day I dug up products from old magazines and talked about all their possibilities. Over meals, I spoke about the road, the sunsets, the heady feeling of not knowing what was out there—glory or disaster.

Could my mother have landed a job? I don't know. After twenty-two years and 246,000 miles, I had almost as much invested in her madness as she.

One morning, after we'd spent half the night reminiscing about old times—our Dreamaway days, the summer we'd roamed Utah with Geiger counters hoping to make a fortune in uranium, the extraordinary night she'd thought up her aphrodisiac empire—it occurred to me that all I'd done was get myself totally confused. My own life—work, laundry, home—began looking paltry and pedestrian. That night I dreamed I was touring grade school children through the tiny rooms of my apartment (light was leaking under all the cracks and jambs), saying that if this clapboard wall weren't here, they'd see the North Star, if that stucco ceiling weren't there, they'd see Venus. I awoke with a jolt. The sun was up. My mother was already at the kitchen table, chewing on a pencil and leafing through the want ads (so far, she had not been able to get herself to circle even one ad, let alone make a phone call). I poured myself a cup of coffee, shambled past her out the screen door and flopped in the sun. After a while my mother came out and joined me. We both adjusted our lawn chairs, slipped on our sunglasses, and tilted our faces toward the sky. But just before I lapsed into a heat-induced torpor, I rolled over and saw her, sitting up now, a leaf of the want ads scuttling off her lap, her feet planted in the sand, squinting out at the desert, looking more lost and bewildered than I was.

Then a letter arrived (forwarded by the television studio) addressed to Gloria c/o *What's My Line?* and scribbled in a blunt pencil:

Dear Gloria,
   I saw you on my tv. Please rush me two (2) viles of your perfume as soon as possible so I can meat some girls. If it really works, I will help you sell a lot more here in town.
   Sincerely,
   Leon De Cee
   Mira Loma, Riverside

Then that afternoon, a postcard came:

Dear Madame,
   Yes, I would like to order *one* bottle of perfume. I hope this product will fulfill my desire for love, and drive wild any female. Your help is very much appreciated.
   Manuel Neptune
   Saugus, California

By the next day, my mother's tiny pigeonhole at the post office was crammed with letters:

Dear Mrs. Gloria,
   Enclosed herewith is our payment for 2 bottles of your perfume. The payment belongs to me and a friend of mine named

Sam Cooper and we intend to use it at my address, which is
below. We kindly wait to receive our order and do thank you
and your firm for selling such a product so hard to find.
Yours faithfully,
Eugene Grant and Samuel Cooper
Azusa, California

To Whom It May Concern:
I'm writing on behalf of my brother. The perfume is *not* for
me but for him. I don't need help. My brother is very lonely
and wants to meet someone. I will order more if it works.
[No name]
PO Box 121
Camp Pendleton

Dear Gloria,
I watched you on What's My Line & like what you had to
say. Your ideas made a lot of sense. I'm very interested in using
your perfume. I'm a male & I'm very unlucky in love. Honestly,
I tell you. I'm so unloved & neglected & lost. Would you kindly
rush me your product, please!
Respectfully submitted,
Salman Kenna
Tujunga Pass, San Bernardino

My mother and I could hardly believe it. Tearing open
the envelopes, skimming over the orders, tallying up her
profits, she said she felt like her old self again. She barely
slept that night. She couldn't wait for tomorrow's mail. She
claimed the men's letters made her feel needed. She said
they gave her a purpose in life. I finally came to the reali-
zation that, despite her grandiose dreams, the woman was
actually happy just running her little empire.
That Friday I left her pecking at her adding machine. It

was well past midnight. I sat down on my cot, pulled out my duffel bag and stared at its worn strap. I knew it was time to leave, I just didn't know if I wanted to go.

"Kimmy," she said, tapping on my door a couple of minutes later, "may I come in?"

I shrugged.

She flopped down beside me. "You look like you're packing."

I nodded.

"Darling, I know you've heard this a zillion times before and I wouldn't blame you if you threw me out of your room—"

"Mom, it's not my room anymore."

"Whatever. But the fact is, I'm on a roll again and more than anything, I want to share it with you."

I rested my temple against a cold rivet in the metal wall and closed my eyes.

"Okay. All right. I know what you're thinking, Kimmy— 'Oh, God, help me, help me, here she goes again.' But this time it's different. I'm different. Look at me—"

I looked at my mother, her right foot tapping, her chewed nails absently picking the lacquer off my bedstand, her eyes rapt and holding within the heart of each glassy pupil the reflection of my night lamp in miniature, its filament glowing.

"I'm not the same dreamer I was. I see things in perspective now. I'm not promising you empires anymore, or riches, I'm just asking you to consider becoming my partner in a stable mail order business that I believe has a solid future."

I began raking my hand through my hair.

"And I'm not just doing this because you're my daughter.

I honestly believe that between you and me, kid, with my
street smarts and pragmatic skills and your brains and education and experience—"

"Mom, I majored in biology. I'm a tour guide in a planetarium."

"That's just my point, darling. I want more out of life
for you than that. We're not talking an apprenticeship here,
we're talking a full fifty-fifty partnership. You don't have to
give me your answer tonight. Just think about it. Maybe
you can come up with a new way to produce and market a
women's pheromone perfume. I don't want you to waste
your education. Use your scientific skills. Women aren't as
gullible as men. It could be your own line. I'd be willing to
run the day-to-day operations and . . . oh, I don't know,
Kimmy, just think about it."

As soon as she left, I wanted to get up and start packing—
escape while I could—but I found myself immobilized on
my cot, staring out the louvered window. Sand was blowing
against the warped slats. A paper plate hurtled by. I could
feel the room buck under my socked feet. Suddenly I wanted
to leave her with something, even if it was only a new
women's line. I flopped back on my bed and, for one insane
moment, I actually did try to break down, in scientific terms,
what the feminine side of desire was. I envisioned the daisy
chain of chromosomes I'd studied in school. I pictured the
unabashed look of hankering I'd seen in women's eyes. I
picked up one of her old tabloids and skimmed through the
personals—"Christian Lady, 47, loves Jesus, water sports,
and children, looking for Christian Guy."

I climbed under the covers and read one of my mother's
old ads: HOW WOULD YOU LIKE TO GET TO FIRST BASE EVERY
time??? EVEN IF YOU'RE SHORT, FAT, BALD, OR OLD, JUST

LET HER GET A WHIFF OF YOU AND WATCH OUT FOR SOME REAL ACTION!!! DOOR-TO-DOOR SALESMEN REPORT LITERALLY BEING DRAGGED IN BY FRUSTRATED HOUSEWIVES (AND INCREASED SALES)! MILITARY SERVICEMEN CLAIM OUTSTANDING SUCCESS WITH LOCAL LADIES! HUSBANDS DESCRIBE INCREDIBLE PERFORMANCES WITH PREVIOUSLY BORED WIVES! INSTANT VIRILITY IN A BOTTLE!!! 100% SUCCESS WITH THE LADIES (IF YOU KNOW WHAT I MEAN) . . . I closed my eyes, trying to imagine what the female equivalent would be.

In the morning, before my mother awoke, I walked down to Searchlight's post office, a white adobe box near an automobile graveyard. If I couldn't come up with a new women's line, I was hoping to at least hand her a fat stack of orders when I gave her the news of my leaving. Her pigeonhole contained three. I started back up the hill and— why should I deny it? I am my mother's daughter—I couldn't wait to read them. "Dear Gloria: Please rush me . . ." "Dear Gloria: Does it really work? . . ." "Dear Gloria:"

I was home with a bout of flu when I saw you on TV. You looked terrific. I must say, I wasn't at all surprised to see you stump the What's My Line panel—no one could ever outguess you, Gloria. Congratulations.

I think about you and Kim often. Those months we spent together now seem like a dreamed interlude in an otherwise ordinary man's life. I hope you've forgiven me for taking off as I did. If you ever find yourself in a jam, or if Kim needs anything, my address and phone number are below—please don't hesitate to call. I would have written sooner but, try as I did, with all your aliases, Gloria, I couldn't find you. Be sure to give Kim my very warmest regards.

Arthur

The oddest thing happened. When I first started reading his letter, I was walking along the Cyclone fence by Searchlight's scrapyard, and now I was a hundred yards out of town, sitting on a rock with no idea of how I got there. I smoothed his letter over my knees and slowly reread it, and next thing I knew, I was still sitting but the rock had been replaced by our trailer's top step, and my mother was holding the letter now, and I was straining to read it over her shoulder, through the wisps of her windblown hair.

Chapter Ten

"Hey, it's no problem, Kimmy," my mother said. "The partnership was only a suggestion. I didn't even know if the net profits could support both of us in the lifestyle we're accustomed to."

She was leaning on the fender of my Volkswagen, absently picking at its mud-flecked guard. I hugged her goodbye, engulfing her ribs, her pop-over housecoat, even the irksome strands of her blowing hair.

"Probably not," I said, sliding into the driver's seat.

Licking her handkerchief, she wiped off the thin film of grit dulling my side-view mirror, leaving the stain of her saliva as a momentary rainbow.

"The women's line probably would have been a bust anyhow," she sighed.

"Probably," I said.

"You shouldn't count on anything, Kimmy. You haven't seen him in years."

I did a double take—we hadn't even talked about my seeing him.

"I mean, what woman in her right mind would fall for one of my ads?"

"None that I can think of, Mom."

She stole a glance at my dashboard clock. "Well, I've got a lot to do. My customers are—"

"You don't have to wait for my car to warm up."

"Hey, thanks, Kimmy," she said.

I watched her in the side-view mirror as she disappeared down the gravel-strewn road on her way to the post office. The sun was at its zenith and she was treading upon her own tiny shadow.

I sped through a dust storm, past The Gold Strike, under the bowed eucalyptus windbreaks with their silver-and-taupe leaves. In the midday heat, my oil gauge skirted red, my steering wheel turned searing. I washed up in a greasy filling station outside of Barstow, fixed my hair at the Victorville rest stop, took one last peek at myself in the Bullock's powder room a couple of miles from his home. Then, crawling along the suburban streets of Calabasas, I pulled up to the curb near his house.

My engine ticked loudly.

For a couple of minutes I scrutinized the place for traces of a new family: a feminine sweep to his living room drapes, a second car, even a tricycle wheel jutting out of the shrubbery. I needed to prepare myself. Dusk was beginning to saturate his yard.

Then I glimpsed his shadow, or what I thought was his

shadow, cast for a second on the foyer's rippled glass: it could just as easily have been a passing cloud.

I felt the blood banging in my ears. I rubbed my neck to calm down. Then, studying myself in the rearview mirror, I combed my hair for the umpteenth time, swung open the car door, stepped into an oily puddle, dried my shoes vigorously on his crabgrass, ambled up his walkway and rang the bell.

"Hi!" I said.

"Kimberly?"

In that instant I took in many things: his graying hair, new creases under his eyes, his not being quite as tall and broad as I remembered. And for a moment I was stunned— you know the sensation: you return to the house of your childhood and it's not as big and bright as the mental blueprint you'd held dear.

To conceal my disappointment, I kissed him on the cheek.

"My God, Kimberly?" he said, shaking his head in wonder and welcome.

"We got your letter," I said as casually as I could, as if that explained why, only four days after he posted it, I'd sped two hundred and sixty miles through the baking desert and a dust storm to show up on his doorstep, uninvited, after six years.

"Actually," I added, as if this might further clarify my presence, "Mom got your letter." I noticed he was holding his car keys. "Really, if you were going out, I could come back another time."

"Kim, please. Don't be ridiculous. Come in, come in."

He led me into his living room, and helped me off with my blue jean jacket (I could feel the brush of his fingertips

on the back of my neck), and suddenly he looked exactly
like my old Arthur.

I wandered around the room, pretending to take in the
knickknacks. He leaned against a bookcase, his head inclined against the walnut wood inlay, watching me.

"Can I get you something to drink?"

"Scotch?"

"A-a-ah, I'm afraid I'm out."

"Wine?" I said. "Or tea? Or coffee or whatever. Really,
tap water would be fine."

He laughed. "Kim, which would you like?

"Tea," I said.

"Tea it is." And he started into the kitchen, stopped,
turned to look at me again before disappearing through the
swinging doors. I heard him making a phone call, speaking
in a low voice, saying that something had just come up at
the office, that he wouldn't be able to make dinner tonight.

I slumped onto the sofa. The house smelled identical to
his old one—Pine-Sol and tobacco mingling with a whiff of
cologne. Under my tapping foot, the familiar shadows of
bamboo blinds played on the carpet, like the stippled shadows sunlight casts on the surface of the ocean when you're
looking up from its depths, from within its unbearable pressure.

"Hey, Kim"—he nudged open the kitchen door—"are you
hungry?"

I hadn't eaten all day; I was ravenous.

"Not necessarily," I said.

"Do you still like Fig Newtons?"

I said I hadn't had one in years, that I was touched he
remembered, and he returned with a platter of cups and
cookies. I spent an inordinate amount of time preparing my

tea, dunking my bag, trolling it back and forth, stirring the tincture of leaves round and round in the water. Arthur leaned against the arm of the sofa, smoking a cigarette. He didn't take his eyes off me.

"So, tell me, Kim, how have you been?"

"Fine," I said, "fine."

"And your mother? How's Gloria?"

"Mom's exactly the same."

"She looked very good on TV. Although she seemed a bit subdued. Is she still as . . . ?"

"Intense?"

He smiled. "Really, I couldn't tell."

"Only last weekend, Arthur, she didn't sleep for two whole nights because she thought she'd figured out a way to capitalize on her *New What's My Line?* success by starting a new line."

"What's Gloria up to now?"

"She wants to make her big comeback by adding a super-strength aphrodisiac perfume. Although, these days, she's much more cautious about what she advertises. She ran into a little difficulty with the Food and Drug Administration. They almost nabbed her for selling a weight loss machine that hooks up to a vacuum cleaner."

Arthur started to laugh: he hugged his ribs and laughed. Then, wiping his eyes with the heels of his hands, he bit back a smile (a gesture so familiar to me I almost touched his knee).

"And Gloria always thought it would be the postmaster general who'd catch her. I guess she's through with that obsession."

"Arthur, in her old age, she actually speaks kindly about him."

"In her old age, does she ever mention me?"

"Often."

"And you, Kim, do you ever . . . ?"

I stared into the depths of my teacup, at its murky dregs. "Why did you leave?" I asked.

"Kim, please, it was a long time ago."

I said I had to know.

He looked at me intently, curiously. "You know exactly why I left," he said.

I was suddenly embarrassed and fifteen again, and to my abject regret, I found myself easing my awkwardness by changing the subject.

"I went to college."

It took him a puzzled moment to follow my non sequitur. "Great," he said softly.

"Majored in biology."

"That's terrific, Kim, really."

"And I'm working at a planetarium now." I didn't mention I was only a tour guide.

"Sounds like you're doing fine."

"Actually, I'm shopping around for even bigger and better prospects"—at that moment, had I been given the option, I would have voluntarily vanished from the world, left it without so much as a trace of my ever having existed.

Arthur laughed. "You know, you sounded just like your mother then."

I blushed deeply, then stared down at the carpet. "I don't know what's come over me, I'm terribly nervous," I said.

"Kim, it's okay, really. I meant it as a compliment. How about a glass of wine?"

"I'd love one."

I followed him into the kitchen, all Formica and shine

like his old one. He stood in the cold, blue-white light of the open Frigidaire, his left hand splayed on the freezer door, his throat lit from below. Through the thin fabric of his white shirt, I could see the outline of his sleeveless T-shirt, the taut shape of his outstretched arm.

"White or red?"

"It doesn't matter."

"Kim?"

"White."

He poured us a couple of glasses of wine. I knocked back mine and asked for another. He looked at me quizzically, then refilled my glass. I sat down on the window ledge, resting my cheek against the cool jamb.

"Arthur," I asked after taking another huge sip, "has everything been okay in your life, I mean with your work and everything?" I didn't dare ask about anything else.

"It's been fine, Kim." He perched on the sill beside me. "I've got my own design firm now."

"That's great, really, congratulations!"

And he told me about an airplane he was building, a test model that rose straight up off the ground without a runway, without velocity or the shudder and tug of speed. "Maybe we could ask your mother to think of a name for it?"

I laughed a little too loudly, then quickly drained the rest of my wine, while Arthur talked about old times; nothing spectacular—the morning we saw the brush fire, the day we planted my mother's Tiki.

We fell silent.

Closing my eyes for a moment, I grew hallucinatorily aware of everything—the brush of his cotton sleeve against my skin, the wine surging in my temples, a last spoke of sunlight warming the windowpane behind us.

"Would you like to have dinner?" he asked.

I looked up at him. The room began spinning in gentle gyrations. My brain was not functioning. I tried to explain that I'd love to have dinner but I had to be at work tomorrow. I still had five hours to drive.

"Kim"—he laughed—"listen to me. I really don't think you should drive right now."

He walked me back into the living room. The shag carpet appeared to undulate under my sandals. We tried to make light of my wooziness. We sat on the sofa, my head on his shoulder, for quite some time. Finally, I couldn't keep my eyes open any longer. I said I had to lie down.

"I ruined our evening, didn't I?" I asked, letting my head sink back on the cushions.

"It's okay, really."

"Arthur, I feel like an idiot."

"These things happen," he said quietly. But I thought I heard a slight irritation in his voice.

I wanted to ask him if he still liked me, but didn't dare.

While he was fetching me a pillow and blanket, I laid my cheek against the bolster and passed out.

When I woke up, I was completely discombobulated. My temples throbbed. My eyelids felt like cardboard. The house had grown dark save for a chink of light emanating from his room. I slipped on my sandals and padded toward it, careful not to make a sound. Stretched out on his bed, Arthur was asleep with his reading lamp on, his left hand shielding his eyes, a book open on his chest. The light was aimed at the pages, at the center of his ribbed T-shirt. The rest of him was barely visible in the jumbled shadows. I had no idea if he'd been waiting up for me. With my blood banging in my ears, I stood over him, trying to figure out what I should do. A faint dusting of black hair silhouetted the rim of his forearm. I could make out the packed shape of his shoulder, the hollow of his underarm with its cloud of black hair, a vein ticking on the side of his neck. The book rose and fell with his breath. Taking a step backward into the shadows, I peeled off my tank top, stepped out of my jeans. Then, with exquisite care, I placed my knee very lightly on the edge of the mattress; next I placed the full weight of my being on that knee until it felt as if I'd tilted the world in my direction.

Arthur blinked open his eyes. "Kim," he said softly, trying to see me through the bright rings of light.

I put my fingers over his lips and, dousing the lamp, climbed onto the bed and pressed my body against his.

Even though he was holding me tenderly in sleep, I had no idea what he thought of me now. I would have loved to slip out, escape from under the pressure of his arms and hit the road again. Simultaneously I didn't want to go. I could hear him breathing deeply, the ticking of the alarm clock, the thudding of my heart. Pressing my face into the hollow of his arm, I tried to glut myself with intimacy of his smell— whereupon, after lying awake for what seemed like hours, I finally turned over and rolled off to sleep.

Then Arthur woke, blinking, cold, sheetless (I had taken the covers). The moon was enormous in the bureau mirror, like a lamp burning in another world, and in those first muddled moments before his memory awoke, he tried to recall exactly what happened: the glasses of wine, putting me to bed on the sofa, the touch and taste of my skin. He propped himself up on his pillow and looked at me (huddled under the covers, on the far side of his bed) and, for a moment, he was filled with a tenderness he hadn't experienced in years. He moved closer, seeking my body again. Through the veil of sheets, he could make out the rise of my hips, the curve of my breast flattened ever so slightly against the stiff mattress. Arousal, like a shot of amphetamine, surged through him. Easing himself up onto his elbow, he carefully peeled back the covers, catching sight of himself in the bureau mirror—his graying head next to my young tanned skin, the ghost of a bikini strap left on my shoulder, my tiny childlike hands with chewed fingernails unconsciously clinging to the top sheet. Closing his eyes, he let his head sink back onto the pillows. A breeze wafted in through the window. I curled up, chilled, shivering in sleep. He covered us again, rested his brow on my shoulder, and whispered calming words into my ear, lulling only himself to sleep.

I was already awake by then, listening as his voice drifted from soothingness into gibberish and breath. I could feel his jaw against my arm. I didn't dare fidget or twitch. I didn't want to wake him again, I just wanted to lie next to his sleeping body for as long as I could. The alarm clock was set for dawn. Light was already sliding up the window blinds. I pressed my face against his chest, trying to blot out the world, and kept it there a long time.

When the alarm trilled, we both sat up. The room was shot with red light. Arthur leaned over and put his hand on my cheek. He did not caress it, he simply pressed his hand against my skin. Then I got up to hunt for my clothes: my jeans were balled on the floor, my sandals strewn under the coverlet. He asked me if he could make me breakfast. I said I didn't have time. He wanted to know if he could at least fix me toast. I shook my head. I suddenly felt like crying because we seemed to have nothing to say to each other. He slipped on his striped pajama bottoms and quickly heated up yesterday's coffee for me. I swigged it down while lacing up the straps of my gladiator sandals.

When the last rawhide knot was looped, I said I guessed I should probably get going, hit the highway before rush hour. I don't know what I expected him to do. Perhaps beg me to stay.

At the front door, he held me against him and asked me to call him soon.

I said of course. My ear was pressed against his sternum; my voice sounded as if it were coming from inside a cave.

Once in my car, barreling onto the freeway, the blacktop shimmering ahead, I began to feel like my old self again, almost relieved to have gotten this over with. The night sky was disappearing behind me with a quick infusion of platinum and azure. My windows were cranked down. All I was conscious of was the roar of speed, the claps of wind when gigantic trucks vied for my lane.

Then, somewhere just over the Big Tehachapi Wash, when my odometer shifted from sixes to sevens, I suddenly felt as if the floor of my world had dropped out and I was falling. I pulled onto the shoulder, braking amid the beer cans and wind-flattened weeds, resting my forehead on the steering wheel, closing my eyes. For a moment I was tempted to go back—not to show up on his wicker doormat or anything, just to park down the street from his house to see him again.

I sat there, being bucked in the wake of semi-rigs. The sun was beating down on my windshield, ricocheting off the dash, but I didn't roll into the shade. I didn't seem to be able to release my foot from the brake. Finally, when the heat and the trucks and the fumes and my despondency had grown unbearable, I veered into traffic again and drove home.

Around eleven I phoned the planetarium with some cock-amamy story about being stuck at a gas station in Fresno. Then, climbing into bed, I pulled the covers up to my chin and fixed my gaze on the ceiling.

Chapter Eleven

Arthur was also staring at his bedroom ceiling, arms folded behind his head, trying to unpuzzle, in the languid heat of the morning, what to make of my visit: my bashful appearance on his doorstep, the brazen way I had come to his bed, the shy and urgent manner in which I'd made love—as though someone might suddenly knock at the door. He lit a cigarette and a ring of blue smoke enveloped the memory. Then he thought about all the work he had to do and got up. Without showering, he headed into his den office, unrolled a blueprint and scrutinized the geometry of yesterday's revisions—the ranks of valves inside the air compressor, the ill-conceived shape of his new turbohead. Within minutes, the hallucinatory clarity of last night, while not losing its charm, faded from his thoughts. Leaning on his elbows, he drew several quick thumbnail sketches of ideal turbines—the comic-book rocket-ship shapes of his youth—and studied them, absently tapping the soft lead of his drafting pencil until it snapped off. Sighing (he did this

half a dozen times a day), he slid off his stool and wandered
back into his bedroom, searching for a box of replacements.
My pillow had not been touched and he walked up to it,
laying his hand in the impression of my head. He glanced
at his watch. I should have been in Oakland by now. He
was tempted to call and started toward the wall phone, but
stopped himself, not wanting to make more of this than it
was. Besides, there was still the mess with Gloria. Finally
he returned to his blueprint but the valves and the lines
and the French curves looked nonsensical. He put his head
on the desk and closed his eyes.

Around one he drove down the hill to his office, picked
up the mail, distractedly chatted with his part-time secre-
tary, closed the glass doors, stared at his phone, paced back
and forth, straightened his already immaculate desk, composed a pointless memo to his assistant, hunted and killed
a horsefly with one deft wallop of a ruler, studied his phone
again, and finally dialed a woman friend asking her to dinner
(anything to put last night in perspective).

He did not get home until after midnight, exhausted and
a little drunk, abandoning the car at the top of the driveway.
His house hadn't cooled off yet, the rooms felt thick, the
rafters ticked and expanded. He unknotted his tie and,
cracking open a couple of windows, headed into his bedroom,
peeling off his white shirt, flopping back on the mattress,
listening to the metronome of his house pulling apart above
him a millimeter at a time. His hall light was on and he
shielded his eyes with the weight of his arm, lapsing into a
momentary oblivion before remembering, with visceral lu-
cidity, the sensation of my presence in his room last night.
For a moment he couldn't tell if it was a night dream or a
daydream or both, but he watched with optical clarity, on

the back on his closed lids, the silhouette of my body moving through the bright rings of his reading lamp. He got up and lit a cigarette, wandered into the living room, poured himself another drink. Resting his head against the window jamb, he stared out at nighttime suburbia—the pale halos of streetlamps, the square of a garage light, the cerulean-blue TV's—and for some reason, he remembered the night of the accident, how he'd sped out of the driveway in a pointless rage over his wife's ridiculously pointless death and accidentally plowed into our trailer, and those hallucinatory months we'd spent together. He wondered if I'd call. There was always the possibility. He had no idea if he really wanted me to.

Knocking back his drink, he tried to put everything out of his mind again, knowing that by the end of the week, it probably wouldn't matter anyway, the whole episode would have faded.

But a week went by and it did not fade. The memory became a little blurrier—as if by constantly examining it, he'd rubbed part of it away—but no less compelling.

He had the nagging feeling that if he could just tell someone about me, this longing would be quelled—but he couldn't imagine who. All his close friends were women, ex-lovers to be exact (he felt stiff and uncomfortable in the company of men) and, stretching out on his sofa, he went over their names—the women he knew, the women he had known. Ironically, the only one he could have talked to about a situation like this was Gloria.

He looked at the clock. It was two A.M. He closed his eyes for a moment, wondering what in God's name he was doing.

On Friday morning he decided to drive up the coast (he

wasn't getting anywhere at work anyway); if and when he got to Oakland, he'd figure things out. He could always not call, or call saying he was in San Francisco on business, just checking in to see that I'd gotten home okay, or something to that mad effect.

At a noisy filling station outside Salinas, he stopped the car. It was four in the afternoon. His back hurt. He hadn't eaten since breakfast. He was hot and tired and annoyed with himself, almost annoyed with me.

Across the asphalt stood a red Coke machine and a glass phone booth. He let his gaze rest on the glass phone booth— it was catching the glare of the late afternoon sun like a block of ice. He had no idea what the point was of putting this off any longer.

He marched across the blacktop, fitted himself into the stifling booth (as hot as ice is cold) and dialed my number.

Three hours later, Arthur stood under the harsh glare of my bald fluorescent hall light, holding a bottle of white wine in one hand and a bottle of seltzer in the other. He smiled shyly. He looked haggard. We came together like lovers who had never kissed before. Then I, who'd barely slept all week either, invited him inside and watched him look around and for the first time ever, I saw my apartment—the world I thought I'd built separately from my mother—with the cold appraisal of another's eye. Save for half a dozen houseplants, I'd decorated the place exactly like her trailer—from the wax paper curtains to the unpacked cardboard box, strewn with old magazines, serving as a coffee table.

Nervously, I picked up the magazines. I said I was still getting situated. I hadn't had a chance to fix things up yet.

"No, no, it looks nice, really," Arthur said. He wandered over to the bay window and stood in the last oblique bars of waxy daylight. "Should I open the bottle of wine?"

I said I'd prefer seltzer and went to fetch us two glasses from an ill-matched set of Texaco stemware (housewarming gift from Mom) and fruit cocktail cups (they'd come free with the jarred fruit).

Arthur poured the seltzer. "Say when."

"When," I said.

The seltzer hissed loudly in the cocktail cups and we clinked rims and suddenly I began to cry. I couldn't stop myself. I tried to turn away but Arthur cupped my head in his hands and held me against him. "What is it?" he asked. "What's wrong?"

I stared into the dark threads of his sweater. I said I didn't think he was ever going to call.

"Kim, please. I didn't know if you wanted me to. You should have told me."

I said I'd already used up my quotient of bravery just showing up at his door.

For a couple of minutes neither of us spoke or moved. We just stood, silent and spent, leaning against one another. Then Arthur put his hand on my breast, through my rayon-ribbed T-shirt. He did not caress it, he simply pressed his hand against me, and I led him to my narrow foam rubber mattress and we made love. It's amazing how quickly the world returns afterward—the floor becomes stable, your feet get cold.

Later, as we lay on the foam, I could not stop watching him. He was stretched out on his back with his eyes closed, his hand on his chest, his elbow half submerged in the spongy mattress. I still had his taste in my mouth—as salty and familiar as seawater—and I felt an unbearable urge to tell him how I'd always desired him, ever since I could remember. But I didn't want to terrify him, so I confined myself to asking him humdrum questions.

Was he hungry?

Could I fix him anything?

Did he think it was hot in here?

If I'd been older, would he have stayed?

He laughed. "Kim, I shouldn't be here now."

I could tell by his voice that he was exhausted, that I was keeping him awake. I fell silent, watching the night thicken around us—a blue layer of indoor twilight dissipating into murky gray. Even when I dozed, I was aware of his unconscious weight beside me. And if he stirred or got up, I woke up too, and watched him shambling sleepily to the bathroom or standing by the open window dragging on a cigarette, his naked outline faintly lit by a carousel of moving headlamps.

He was in no way remarkable-looking. His hair was beginning to turn gray, and thin, and he moaned in his sleep, or snored softly, and I was overcome with compassion at the sight of his chest, at the bend of his knees.

And I'd think how remarkable his chest and knees were. I'd think and dream.

By Sunday afternoon it was becoming astonishingly apparent that I didn't want him to go home.

We were sitting up in bed (we'd barely left the apartment all weekend) discussing for the umpteenth time why he had to leave tomorrow—his work, his business, et cetera, et cetera. And even though I knew rationally why he had to get back, the part of me that was my mother saw no reason why the whole world couldn't buckle to fit into my one small dream. So what if he had a business to run? So what if he had employees to pay? Why couldn't he just move the whole kit and caboodle up here?

Pressing his fingers to his temples, he slowly massaged them. Then he took me by the shoulders and tried to say something light and diverting.

I shrugged. I wouldn't be diverted.

He started to justify once again why he had to go home.

I said I understood. I said he didn't have to keep going on and on about it, I wasn't obtuse.

We were both leaning against the wall now. Suddenly he closed his eyes and put his head on my lap. I ran my hands over his face, his throat, his shoulders.

"I don't know what you want of me," he said. "This is just as mysterious to me as to you."

I was holding on to his head now and I wouldn't let go.

"Why don't you just come back with me, Kim." His voice sounded muffled in my lap: I had to strain to hear. "At least for a while. I haven't the slightest idea what will happen. Just come."

My foot had fallen asleep under the weight of his head. I closed my eyes for a moment. I'd already missed the last three out of four weeks at work—I was probably going to be fired anyway. I said, "Hey, it's no problem, I have all this vacation time coming to me." Then I opened my eyes and looked down at him. His face was shadowed by my thigh. I couldn't tell if he already regretted his offer. I gently maneuvered myself free of his bulk and lay down beside him and stroked his back, a caress as proprietary as it was loving.

Next morning, for Arthur's sole benefit, I faked a phone

call to the planetarium requesting time off, then slipped across the hall to ask my neighbor, a skeleton-thin art student with whom I sometimes got high, to water my rubber plants and screen any calls from Mom. Arthur was lugging our suitcases (my khaki duffel bag, his Samsonite overnighter) down the narrow staircase and out to his car.

"Is that the guy you've been telling me about?" she said, watching him close the front door behind him.

I nodded.

"You're kidding."

I wanted to know what she meant by that.

I don't know," she said airily. "I guess it's kind of weird. I mean"—she traipsed over to the front window and cupped her eye to the glass—"he's okay-looking and everything but . . . hey, Kim, I don't know . . . He looks like some guy my father would play golf with or something."

When I got outside, Arthur was waiting on the curb, squinting up at the hazy sky.

"Ready?" he asked, smiling.

"I guess."

He slammed the trunk and opened the car door for me. I slid onto his enormous leather seat.

"Should we stop for some breakfast?" he asked, climbing in beside me.

I shrugged.

"Not hungry?"

I said I was just a little nervous, was all.

A dense fog enveloped us in Big Sur. It looked as if we were driving through wool. Oncoming highbeams flared and disappeared. I fiddled with the radio tuner, dragging it up and down the green dial, not wanting to talk. Then I stared out at the dense emptiness, at the rush of vapor. From time to time a tiny townlet, just halos of dripping streetlights, floated by. At the crest of the mountains, where the highway hung over the gray Pacific, hitchhikers appeared—a whole gauntlet of them, all thumbs and scrawled signs and youth. Their shadows looked like paper cutouts in our yellow fog lamps. When patches of fog swallowed them up again, I actually felt relieved. By Arroyo Grande the hitchhikers gave way to junked automobiles and shreds of rubber retreads scattered along the emergency lane.

We had not spoken in almost an hour. I could tell that Arthur hadn't the slightest idea of what was going on. When we stopped at a hamburger stand near Buellton, he tried to make small talk over the french fries and Cokes. When we parked for a moment at the summit of the Santa Ynez Pass, he watched me quizzically as I feigned interest in the valley-strewn vista.

By the time we pulled up to his house, he seemed completely perplexed by my mood. He left me alone to unpack my duffel bag, while he fixed dinner. He tried to put his arms around me in the bathroom, while I brushed my teeth. He kissed me on the back of my neck, Indian file down my vertebrae, while I lay stiffly in bed. And when he finally gave up and fell sleep, exhausted and confused, I slipped out from under the sheets. I took a pillow and curled up on his living room sofa, staring at its plaid patterns.

After a while, Arthur wandered in, carrying a blanket. He lay down beside me and covered us up.

"Kim, what's wrong?" he asked.

I told him I was a wreck, that I didn't think I could fall asleep on his soft mattress.

"Then we'll sleep on the sofa or drag in a couple of chaise lounges," he said wearily. "Or we could even scale the backyard fence and sleep on my neighbor's pool floats. They were spying on us when we drove up, we might as well give them something to talk about."

I laughed.

You could tell the poor man was relieved.

I asked him if he thought we had a hope in hell.

"Kim, I haven't the faintest idea."

I felt like crying again.

"Are you sleepy?" he asked.

"Not really."

"Try and sleep."

He gently reached over me to extinguish the light and the shadow of his hand fell across my pillow. He noticed me watching it, and with the slightest manipulation of his fingers, he transformed the lifeless shadow into a living animal—a hound, I think—baying at the ever changing moon: the moon was a pair of passing headlamps.

I laughed again.

"I think this was my only talent as a boy," he confessed. And he began to show me his whole repertoire of shadow-graphs—a duck ruffling its feathers, a rabbit scratching its ear, Franklin Delano Roosevelt's profile, a cat licking its paws . . .

Finally I closed my eyes, and burrowing my face into the hollow of his arm, I drifted into a dream where everything was its opposite:

Where the shadows were the body. Where left was right. Where no one went unloved. Where Arthur was young.

Chapter Twelve

So that I might feel more comfortable in his unfamiliar home, in his soft, alien bed, Arthur surprised me next day by lugging in a brand-new plywood board to sandwich between his box spring and mattress. For some reason, this more than anything else—more than our lovemaking or our talking or his fixing me breakfast—touched me deeply. In return, I tried to demonstrate as much commitment as I was capable of by putting my belongings into his drawers, folding them neatly next to his socks. I even allowed him to store my duffel bag out in the garage, up in the rafters, just above my reach.

On Wednesday morning Arthur finally roused himself out of bed, saying that he'd better make an appearance at his office today. He got dressed but he loitered in the foyer, talking to me, kissing me on the neck, pocketing his car keys, then looking for same car keys, stunned by his own absentmindedness. But he could see that I was charmed by it. He headed out to his garage, waved goodbye, then did something totally out of character and strangely moving: he grabbed hold of his necktie (despite its meticulous Windsor knot) and pretended that a being stronger than himself, stronger than any of us, was yanking him toward his car while he struggled to remain with me. A moment later, as if embarrassed by his own boyishness, he shrugged and slid in behind the steering wheel. I followed him to the hem of the driveway, watching him drive off.

Alone in the house, I leafed through magazines, fiddled with the blinds, turned the television set on and off. I poked around the backyard. Then, sometime in the late afternoon, sinking onto the sofa with one thonged foot folded under me, I found myself staring at the phone. It had been weeks since I'd talked to my mother and I knew she'd be desperate to hear from me. I stretched out on the checkered cushions, feeling intense trepidation about calling her and not knowing exactly why. I took a deep breath, pulled the phone an inch or two closer and dialed the trailer.

"Gloria's World of Aphrodisiacs."

"Hey," I said.

"Kimmy!"

I told her where I was.

"In Calabasas?"

"In Calabasas."

"With Arthur?"

"Uh-huh."

"You've been there the whole time?"

I gave her an abridged version of what had happened. "Mom, I'm sorry I didn't call sooner."

"Hey, it's okay, don't worry about it, kid"—I waited for her to switch ears— "I've been around the block myself, I know how these things go."

I could tell by the way she said this that she was hurt.

"Mom, are you okay?"

"I'm just great. Things are really happening fast now. Yesterday I had to bring a pillowcase to the post office just to pick up all my mail. Kimmy, when are you going back to Oakland?"

I said I didn't know yet but I had a feeling I was going to be here for quite some time.

I waited for her to clear her throat.

"Mom, are you sure you're okay?"

"I guess I'm a little shocked, is all. I guess I thought you were just going to see him—okay, maybe even sleep with him, but not move in."

I sank back on the sofa, closing my eyes. "Mom, listen, this is something I need to do."

Her breath on the mouthpiece sounded faint and ragged.

"I just hope that nothing comes between us," she said quietly.

"Mom, nothing's going to come between us."

Another long pause.

"So, do you want to hear a couple of my letters?" she asked.

"Sure," I lied.

"Dear Sir," my mother began. "Hey, Kimmy, I'm just picking these out of the bag at random."

"I understand."

"Dear Sir"—I could almost envision her as she squinted through her new pink bifocals at the crumpled letter with its crabbed illegible handwriting—"Could you please send me the stuff tha' tracks women?"

I laughed.

"Here's another: Dear Gloria. I have always been alone,

though people say I have a good personality. Women are turned off by me because of my large size. Though I am used to living alone and see some benefits to it, I would like to share my life with someone. I don't know why I'm telling you this—a complete stranger—but your product sounds too good to be true. I know there are a lot of scams out there so please don't let me down. I'm a good man, I deserve some happiness too."

"Mom, that's the saddest letter I've ever heard."

"I've got a whole pillowcaseful. You want to hear more?"

"Not right now."

"Kimmy, are you sure you know what you're doing?"

"Mom, please."

"Will you call me soon?"

I said I would call her soon and we hung up.

I flopped back on the cushions. I draped my arm over my eyes to blot out the world. I couldn't move.

Twenty minutes later the phone rang.

"You know, I was just thinking," my mother began—her voice sounded a fraction of a tone shriller, a decibel more vulnerable. "Kimmy, how long did you say you were going to be there?"

"Mom, I didn't say. For a while at least."

"Because in a couple of weeks I've got an appointment in your area with one of my customers who sells commercial time on satellite TV."

"Oh God, Mom, please don't come just yet."

Long pause. I could hear her clearing her throat again, the blast of a semi-tanker's horn somewhere in the distance.

"Hey, don't worry about it," she said finally.

"You sure, Mom? You understand?"

"As I said, kid, I've been around the block a few times, I know how these things go."

I shut my eyes. I waited a beat. I knew by the way she'd said this that she hadn't the slightest inkling of why I didn't want her to come.

"So," I said with forced levity, "let's hear all about satellite TV."

"You're really interested?"

"You bet."

"Kimmy, can I ask you something?"

"Of course."

"Do you think I gave you enough stability as a kid? I mean, aside from all the moving and everything . . . oh, you know what I mean."

"Mom, you were . . . are a terrific mom."

She began telling me the benefits of satellite TV.

Arthur walked in, kissed me on the back of my neck, then motioned to the taut phone cord and looked at me curiously.

I cupped my palm over the speaker. "Mom's on the line," I explained, "talking about the benefits of satellite TV." I rolled my eyes comically. "She's even hinting that she wants to come visit."

Arthur wandered over to the window and lit up a cigarette. He looked extremely tense.

I said, "Hey, Mom, this call is costing you all your profits. Why don't I phone you back?"

"You won't be long, Kimmy? I'm on a tight schedule."

"I'll just be a sec."

I gently cradled the receiver and walked over to Arthur. He was standing in a haze of blue smoke. I rested my brow against his sleeve.

"Kim," he said quietly, "I don't think I'm ready for this."

"Listen, she's not coming. She's just . . . oh, come on, Arthur, you know my mother."

I suddenly felt an unbearable tug between them. For a moment I just stood there, breathing in the scent of his cigarette, not knowing what to do. "Arthur," I said finally, "she's expecting my call. You okay?"

"I'm just fine. Really. Go ahead."

"You sure?"

He nodded.

I padded upstairs and dialed the trailer.

"Okay," my mother continued midsentence, "I see myself expanding. And that's where satellite TV comes in—"

I could hear Arthur downstairs, pacing. When I closed my eyes, I could picture my mother tramping back and forth in her tiny trailer, slightly flushed from excitement, the wind and all the wind's relics—sand, bubble gum wrappers, paper plates—relentlessly hurtling by.

"You see, what I've finally come to realize, Kimmy, what my TV appearance has taught me, is that all my life I've been constrained too tightly by real space slash time perimeters. And what are those, after all?" my mother asked.

I heard the back door open and close. I carried the phone to the window, pressing my cheek against the screen. The patio was pitch-black. I couldn't see Arthur but I could see the tip of his cigarette leaving a firefall of sparks as he dragged on it.

"Outside these dimensions," my mother went on, "there'll be no stopping me. With global technology, I can bounce my messages, my ads, Kimmy, off the satellites and be able to reach—"

I shut my eyes again and lowered the receiver. My mother's tiny voice reached me anyhow.

". . . Seattle or Paraguay or Ohio or New Delhi or Rome or Bakersfield or Calabasas . . ."

That evening, Arthur fixed dinner and we ate quietly at the kitchen table, barely glancing up from our plates. I could hear the ping of our forks, the scrape of our soup spoons against the sides of the bowls. We got undressed on opposite sides of the bed, then read—facing the reading lamps, our backs to each other. The instant we turned off the lights, however, I sensed that Arthur was watching me.

"Kim, are you awake?"

I was staring up at the ceiling, a mysterious plane of phantasmagorical dimensions in the moonless night.

"I think we should talk," he said.

I didn't want to talk. I pretended to be on the brink of sleep.

"I know you're awake, Kim. Please . . . I've got to talk to you." I could feel him shift his weight, rest his forehead against my shoulder. "It's about your mother and me. It's not important. I mean, it happened a long time ago. I just don't want you to hear it from—"

I rolled over. I said, "Arthur, I already know what you want to tell me, I just don't want to hear it out loud."

Then I shut my eyes. I sensed that he was about to speak again, so I did the only thing I knew how to do to stop him— I seduced him. There was safe refuge in our lovemaking and I wanted to enter it now, as one enters and hides in a dark closet.

Hours later, when I was sure he was fast asleep, I crept across the mattress and nestled against him again. His body felt stiff, almost rigid and crimped in dreams. His face looked tense on the white pillow. I held him tightly and by telepathy, or by dream communication, or by the sheer pressure of my cells and pores against his, I tried to explain to him that I'd always known about my mother and him, and that for some inexplicable reason, it simply didn't matter to me. What I wanted from this point forward was just to be able to be with him.

Chapter Thirteen

By the end of the month, we gave up the pretense of my keeping my own place in Oakland. We rented a U-Haul and towed my boxes and books down the Grapevine. Whenever we passed an old trailer park where Mom and I had once lived, I made sure not to point it out—I didn't want her name always cropping up between us. But during the long drive home, between the ceaseless wind, and the familiar parks, and seeing an old woman walking along the shoulder of the highway, I couldn't get her out of my mind. Even as I began to adjust to my middle-class life with Arthur—sharing socks and T-shirts, arguing about who vacuumed last, or lying side by side in bed at night hushed and content—I knew she was out there alone. Sometimes there'd be moments, just before we'd drift off to sleep, when I'd catch the roar of the freeway and suddenly the walls of our cozy house would drain of color, like blood from a face, and I'd be racing toward her over a desolate stretch of highway to an unmarked place on the horizon where glory and dust intersect.

I'd sit up with a jolt, then quietly, so as not to awaken Arthur, slip out from under our tumble of sheets and pad over to the window. My heart would be pounding. Invariably Arthur would sense something was awry and get up and try to comfort me, but as worried as I was about my mother, I couldn't verbalize why.

On the surface, she was doing great. Her *What's My Line?* publicity was paying off. She'd finally left Searchlight for good. She was having a fling with a trucker. But most important, she was beginning to view her life again through the filtered lenses of her old Technicolor dreams. She even talked about rekindling studio interest in the movie version of her life story. Not just for the publicity, she said, but because she honestly felt there was an important moral lesson in her tale, although she wasn't quite sure what that lesson was. At night, when her perfume orders had been mailed out and the money counted, she'd lie on her chaise lounge, washed in moonlight, and see her whole life playing out on the dome of the sky. Every scene—from the knobby-kneed first-grader to the industrious entrepreneur—would be tinged with the mystery of accomplishment and all its special effects. Then the moon would dip behind a cloud and her vision, or whatever you want to call it, would slowly dissolve.

She worked Nevada for a while. Arthur and I got post-cards from Silverpeak, Midas, Goldfield, and Vegas. Unable to afford extensive advertising, let alone satellite commercials, she finagled a young journalist into mentioning her perfume in his health and beauty column, gave out free samples at bowling alleys and driving ranges, and in a moment of sheer inspiration, charmed a local radio talk show host into granting her an interview.

"We're on the air with entrepreneur Gloria Gail. Spray-and-tell time, callers. Sexual attraction in an aerosol? Come on, Gloria. Birds do it, bees do it, but *humans?*"

"Absolutely," my mother said. "Think about it. Why else does a woman desire one man and not another? Can an inch or two of height, a few years more or less, a receding hair-line, make *that* much difference? I don't think so."

The phone lines lit up.

Two nights later, speeding between Sparks and Reno, she turned on her car radio and suddenly heard her own voice—a little nasal and nervous, but choked with conviction—filling the cabin, and she had to pull over into the emergency lane, just to listen in awe at the strangeness of it all. The moon was suspended above her rumbling hood. Gusts of hot wind, shot with a vague iridescence, blew by. She cranked down her window and took in the desert air.

Her empire now extended from Truckee to Yuma, from Lake Pyramid to the gray Pacific. It had never been so extensive. Sitting by a pool at dusk (she was able to splurge on motels these days), she'd take out her road map to plan the next day's conquest and become overwhelmed by the enormity of her achievements.

She decided to trade in the trailer and car on an almost new Cadillac. "I know we talked about my leaving it to you someday, Kimmy, but the fact is, I'm on a roll now and the cumbersome thing is just slowing me down."

In a snapshot she mailed us, she was sitting on the hood of her new cream-colored Caddy, her head thrown back, her hair flying, one hand on the padded shoulder of a short, blushing customer, the other holding up, for all the world to see, the thousandth bottle of perfume sold that summer. Sunlight was striking the golden liquid, throwing prismatic glints on her wrist, crepe neckerchief, and radiant smile.

But three nights later, at a Ramada Inn, she found herself snapping at a slow-witted bellhop after closing a sale; the boy had only asked if she could extend her money-back guarantee. The next evening, much to her dismay, she cut short a lonely old regular who used to call as much to hear her raucous voice and flirt as for the perfume: she said she had no time for him now. She hung up, terribly confused and ashamed. After all, these were the men who had made her what she was today. Why was she suddenly acting like this? Maybe it was all the pressure she was under, the exhaustion of the road, but she didn't feel tired. On the contrary, she could rarely sleep.

She rode the elevator down to the swimming pool. She dove in. The pool light illuminated the world below. Everything looked unreal—the tips of her flowing hair, the recesses of the deep end, the silver drain. Reflections of the water scattered and swam up along the tiled walls. Her lungs ached for air, the water pressed against her temples, her ears popped from the pressure: she heard the drone of the filter, the thudding of her heart. And she honestly didn't know the source of her uneasiness. Her initial dream seemed to be ebbing away, leaving her adrift in this sparkling pool, in this empty courtyard.

She realized she needed a change. "I've come to a fork in the fast lane," she wrote us later that night. She said she was going to have to either slow down and return to an easier pace or push on to something larger, perhaps even shoot for her lifelong dream of running a nationwide ad campaign. She made a list of pros and cons—gains versus

debits, risks versus losses, the known versus the unknown—
and asked Arthur and me for our opinion.

At 11:16 she sealed our letter, dropped it down the hotel
mail chute and climbed into bed. At 11:21 three scenarios
began running through her head. In the first, she saw herself ten years from now, her hair peppered gray, driving the
same dusty roads through the same dinky towns, perhaps
in a Mercedes Benz. In the second, it was as if the projector
had gone wild—glass cities loomed and vanished, her ads
appeared in full Technicolor, she traveled by airplane,
streaking across cobalt skies that are always present above
the clouds. In the third, thirty years had passed and she
was very old. From her tweed coat and brown oxfords, she
couldn't tell if she was rich or poor, successful or not, but
it didn't matter. Something about this elderly woman's posture—the way she carried her neck and head—made you
know that this was a woman who had not held back, who
had truly lived.

By 5:33 in the morning, she had decided to risk everything. She stood in front of the chiffon curtains, staring at
the rising sun, pretty sure—no, *very* sure—no, *absolutely
positive* she was doing the right thing. The air-conditioned
air seemed a little crisper, her coffee tasted a little stronger.
Sun came charging through the blinds, displaying resplen-
dent patterns of dust.

That afternoon, on Ramada Inn stationery, she composed
the first of her national ads—a crisp scientific one for *The
Enquirer,* a slightly more earthy one for *The Star,* and three
tiny classifieds for *Real Detective, Guns and Ammo,* and *Pent-
house Letters* respectively. By early October, the first of her
continental orders came in—ten from the Deep South, a
trickle from the Midwest, and over three dozen from Oregon

and Alaska. She restocked immediately. November and December, however, proved much slower and she couldn't figure out why. Maybe it was the holidays or a glitch in the economy? She wasn't going to take chances. She holed up in a motel room, subsisted on coffee, and rewrote her ads, dropping the scientific slant and punching up the mystery factor. But January orders only dribbled in. And without her personal touch, her Nevada regulars began abandoning her one by one (you see, these men weren't drawn so much to her perfume as they were to the scent of her dreams). By February, all that was left of her empire were a few distant outposts—PO boxes and such—scattered on the rim of three states.

"I feel like I'm free-falling without a parachute," she wrote us in late March. But what she didn't mention, because she didn't understand it herself, was that the faster she fell, the closer she came to crashing, the more alive she felt. Sometimes, after going over and over her diminishing accounts, her heart would be racing so fast that the blood in her head would begin to bang and throb like shaken seltzer and she could almost feel the effervescence of imminent danger, the rapture of the deep. Other times, after having plotted and schemed and brainstormed for twenty-four hours straight without the glimmer of a solution, she'd stand by the window, bleary-eyed but still hopeful, watching the sun rise over the hazy desert. The year was 1969 and everyone was talking about the upcoming moon landing and for a while she became obsessed with incorporating *that* fervor into her ads—weightlessness, gravity, the bright streamlined future. If it didn't work for her perfume, she still had an exclusive on her weight loss machines and surely she'd be able to figure out a way to use it there.

Every evening, nursing a last cup of coffee, she'd sit on the chrome bumper of her Caddy, under the huge canopy of the night, convinced that inspiration was about to descend upon her. But it never came.

She began working Nevada again, driving this way and that, eking out a living by selling cut-rate bottles of perfume out of the trunk of her car. There were no special effects now. The road didn't whiz by, there were no quick dissolves, the radio didn't play something catchy (it had stopped working in Boulder). She had to drive the full length of every stifling mile, in the oven-hot cabin, in the dun colors of late afternoon. And when she arrived at a roadside motel, there were no instantaneous cuts that landed her in a sparkling, kidney-shaped pool. She had to check in, drag her suitcase to the far bungalow, unpack, peel off her fishnet stockings, wash them out with sample soap in the basin, drape them over the towel rack, undress, and stretch out on the pilly bedspread, waiting for the droning air condiditoner, and the respite of sleep, to kick in.

She spent sixteen months alone. She put over fifty thousand miles on her Cadillac. She was now staying in motels with names like Kozy Kabins and eating at truck stops and Tasty Freezes. Then, one morning in early July, she called collect to ask if she could swing by to watch the upcoming moon landing with us—maybe it would inspire her again. She even hinted that she'd like to take an R and R on our sofa for a couple of weeks. She acted cavalier, joking about how she could use some of Arthur's home cooking, but I heard the urgency in her voice—and I knew that, despite my trying to hide it, she must have heard the hesitancy in mine.

Arthur and I were still getting adjusted. Alone, we were incredibly happy. A meal together, just shopping at the hardware store for screens, the shape of his forearm on the pillow beside me, still struck me as remarkable. In company, however, we were awkward and uncomfortable. Once, at a dinner party, the wife of a colleague of Arthur's had offered each of her guests the slim stem of a martini glass, then presented me with a mug of milk. Another time, an old college friend of mine had shown up at our door and greeted Arthur as "Pop." I didn't know if I could handle my mom's volatile presence on top of this.

I said, "Hey, Mom, let's meet in Vegas, like in the old days. Just you and me. I'll take you out on the town. I'm making good money now." I was selling scientific equipment to local colleges. "We could watch the moon landing on the giant screen at the Nugget. I'll bet the bookies are taking long shots on some aspect of it."

"I guess whether Neil Armstrong trips or not while taking that first step," my mother said quietly.

"Meeting in Vegas is just an idea, Mom," I said, holding the phone in my fist, secretly praying that she would say yes.

For a sec she didn't say anything.

"Well, I guess it would be okay. Sure. Why not?"

I could hear by the intonations in her voice how deeply disappointed she was.

"Besides, it's probably for the best," she went on. "You never know when business is going to pick up again."

I sank onto the sofa and tilted my head back against the cushions. We both knew that her business wasn't going to "pick up again."

I hung up. I talked things over with Arthur. I called her

back, inviting her to come. I even bought her her first first-class airplane ticket. I figured that if I could sit down and talk with her, I might know what to do.

Three hours before the lunar touchdown, she phoned to say she had both good news and bad. She wasn't going to make the moon landing because one of her suitcases—well, not exactly a suitcase, more like a box she had fastened together with electrical tape—had either been lost or stolen or maybe the fragile thing had just blown apart during the bumpy flight. The point was, it didn't matter. The point was that opportunity had finally knocked again. She was traveling first-class with all the first-class bennies—good food, free champagne, *and* luggage insurance. While she and an airport supervisor were searching for the missing box, her plane had taken off again which was A-okay with her because now they'd probably never find the box. And she couldn't even remember what was in the box anyhow. What she needed from Arthur and me were receipts for "upscale clothes and jewelry and foreign cameras and maybe even golf clubs—"

"Mom, stop. I can't tell if this is the good news or the bad. Where are you?"

She was stuck at the Idyllwild airport. Because of a freak hailstorm no more planes were going out tonight. She needed me to come fetch her by car. She would meet me in Arrivals. She was terribly upset about not getting to watch the moon landing with us and was considering suing the airline for compensation for that as well. Most important, if an insurance representative from the airlines called, we were to tell them she had receipts.

I gently cradled the receiver.

"Is everything all right?" Arthur asked.

"Everything's just fine," I said. "I'm going to pick Mom up at Idyllwild."

"Kim, that's over a three-hour drive. Why can't she take another plane?"

"There are no other planes," I said.

He started to fetch his car keys but I stopped him.

"Arthur, I really think I should go alone."

It was raining in the mountains around Idyllwild—at five thousand feet, icy tumbleweeds like enormous snowflakes began blowing out of the blackness, and by six thousand feet, a brittle sheath of sleet coated the highway and sand. I pulled into the tiny airport behind a hoarfrosted Greyhound bus and parked in its blue exhaust. It was 2:58 in the morning and the place was practically empty, save for half a dozen soldiers and my mother.

She was sitting by herself near the baggage claim carousel, staring intently at a black-and-white pay TV. Her right foot was tapping, her eyes were slit, her hands lay folded in her denimed lap, next to a roll of quarters. I couldn't see what was on but I knew by her spellbound expession that it was the lunar landing. All around her, scattered on the floor by her sandaled feet, were plastic bags, cardboard cartons, a khaki duffel bag, three Samsonite suitcases, and her flamingo-pink makeup purse—not exactly two weeks' worth of costume changes, more like everything she owned.

I crept up behind her, tucking a wisp of her hair behind her ear. "Impressed with the moon landing, Mom?" I whispered.

"Oh, 'impressed' is not the right word, Kimmy," she sighed. "It is remarkable." Without turning around, she patted the seat next to her: her wrist was bangled with copper bracelets, her tan looked as permanent as a tattoo.

I sat down beside her.

"You know," she said, her focus still riveted to the tiny screen, where a windless flag listed on a steel pole near a silver leg of the spacecraft, "you know how I always feel like an outsider, like a Martian, whenever I'm around Americana—"

I said I knew.

"Well, I still feel out of it and I still get nauseous with this whole stars-and-stripes routine, but I have to say, when Neil Armstrong's boot touched lunar dust, I did feel proud to be a Homo sapiens."

"I'm sorry I missed that moment with you, Mom."

"Hey, it's okay, Kim."

We embraced.

Then I huddled beside her and we watched the astronauts perform their weightless minuet on pocked moonscape until her quarters ran out.

I lugged her belongings out to the car.

"Did they ever find your box?" I asked, unlocking her door.

"Huh?"

"Your missing box, Mom. Did they ever find it?"

She absently shook her head, then slid into the passenger seat. She didn't seem interested in her box any longer.

I released the emergency brake and we headed out onto the glassy highway.

"That was truly something, wasn't it, Kim?"

I said it was. I said I didn't mean to change the subject so fast but maybe we should talk about her for a while . . . her future and everything.

"Aren't we on Route Seventy-four?"

"I think so."

"Didn't we used to drive this canyon in the old days on our way to Indio?"

"I guess. Mom, listen to me—"

"Do you remember that night . . . God, it must have been over twenty years ago, Kimmy . . . We were driving through here, probably on this very stretch of highway, and we saw that ring of people, with their telescopes and kids?"

"Mom, I—"

"Their campers and trailers were parked in a circle and they were holding hands."

"Mom, really, I don't remember."

"Oh, come on, Kimmy. You were crazy to join them, because you were just entering a phase where you were obsessed about becoming a Camp Fire girl or a Brownie or something and you hoped these people were the trailer park coalition."

"You know, you're right. I do remember."

"So we pulled over and trudged up to them and they were all certifiably mad."

"I didn't think so."

"Take my word for it, Kim, you were just a little kid. They were a club of UFO aficionados."

I did a double take. "Aren't we being a little hypocritical, Mom? I remember plenty of nights when you scanned the heavens with your Brownie camera after the TV said weird lights had been seen in the area."

"That was purely for financial reasons. Do you know how much the tabloids used to pay for a snapshot of a flying saucer?"

"Come on, Gloria, admit it. You believed!"

"Okay, all right, I was open to the idea, was all. That's just the point I'm trying to make, Kim. May I finish my story?"

I cranked down my window. The cold desert air rushed in. I gulped down a bracing lungful. "Take me back to that night, Mom," I said.

"As I said, the bedlamites were all in a circle, holding hands. And their camper lights were all intersecting, making some sort of weird geometrical configuration. I guess it spelled 'welcome' in Venusian or Jupitarian. You were jumping up and down, you were so excited, and I have to admit, it was pretty difficult not to get caught up in the fervor. I mean, picture thirty upturned faces, all expectant, all hoping to be levitated out of their workaday lives. Well, when I saw the astronauts on the moon tonight, it just ended an era for me. Kimmy, I want to move in with you and Arthur. I mean, I can't kid myself any longer, honey. No one is coming for me."

Chapter Fourteen

I veered into the emergency lane and braked to a bumpy stop. I killed the motor and doused the highbeams. Dawn was coming up in gray gradations, turning the blowing sand into iridescent cinders.

Resting my head against the bucket seat, I turned to my mother. I knew that with her mercurial attention span, I had only a few minutes to make my point and I needed her to understand.

"Mom," I said, "you can't move in with Arthur and me. I'll do anything for you, help you in any way, but—"

"Hey, it was only a suggestion," she said. Her gaze drifted out the window to a tiny pink dust devil hurling its way down the sandy highway. "I've got all kinds of plans brewing and not just the insurance number. I mean, that's just a distraction, Kimmy, to keep me limber until something better comes along."

"Mom, please listen to me. If you need money, I'll give you whatever I can, but while you're staying with Arthur and me, you've got to keep your . . . your business plans to yourself."

"You mean I can never run an idea by you, Kimmy? You know how much I respect you."

"Not me, Mom, you can talk to me." I was already breaking down. "Just leave Arthur out of it. Please."

"Hey, I understand, kid, I really do." She blinked and stared down at the floor. "I am not obtuse."

I turned over the ignition and we drove on in silence. When we got to Calabasas, I began nervously pointing out all the local hot spots—our grocery store, our twenty-four-hour laundromat, our favorite coffee shop—anything to break the silence.

"Just don't go wild with all the nightlife," she said quietly.

I knew this was her own peculiar way of making peace.

I pulled into our garage. "You go on in, Mom. I'll get your bags." I watched her clop hesitantly up the walkway. Then I sat for a moment in the darkness.

By the time I'd dragged in all her boxes and bags, she was sitting on a corner of the sofa—her shoulders hunched, her eyes slit and squinting at the sun-flecked bookcases, then at the red Chinese rug, then at the amber glass coffee table (with tiny reflections of her copper bangle bracelets dancing on top).

"Looks classy," she said. She picked up a marble ashtray, weighed it in her palm, then carefully set it down again. "You even have knickknacks."

I nodded.

Arthur shambled out of our dark bedroom blinking into the sunlight, knotting up his Scotch plaid robe, rubbing his left, sleep-swollen eye with the back of his hand.

"Hello," my mother said, rising to her feet. She had not seen him in almost eight years.

"Gloria." He smiled and looked at her curiously, warmly, a little nervously. "My God, Gloria," he said, shaking his head.

She ran her hand over her flyaway hair.

"You look great."

"Hey," my mother sighed, rolling her eyes up. "Don't kid a kidder. I look like hell." But I could see that she was flattered.

They embraced awkwardly; then stood on either side of me in their new improbable roles, waiting for me to break the tension.

"Anyone for coffee?" I asked. "Boy, I sure could use some."

"None for me," Mom said. She surreptitiously took in Arthur again, then me, then him once more. "Hey, I'm already wired enough. You guys don't happen to have any Valium?"

Arthur laughed. "I'm afraid herb tea is about as close as we get, Gloria."

"Sorry," she said, studying us both again, "I never touch the stuff."

I slipped into the kitchen, put up the percolator and waited for its pop and hiss. Through the open Dutch doors, I could see the blue smoke of Arthur's cigarette, the gauzy dimensions of my mother's fishnetted knees. She had sunk back onto the sofa and was crossing and recrossing her legs, talking to Arthur in an animated whisper.

I drifted toward the open door, listening.

Smoking a cigarette herself, she was telling Arthur about her airport mishap and her lost box and her pressing need for legit, backdated receipts (actually what she needed from him were any sale slips he might have lying around for luxury items that could logically fit into a two-foot-by-three-foot cardboard box). Arthur was listening with bewildered fascination.

I wanted to kill her.

After a while, Arthur wandered into the kitchen, wondering where I was.

"I'm going to ask her to leave," I said. "I'm furious."

"Kim"—he put his arms around me—"what do you want from her? She's scared right now. She's just grasping at straws." He pressed his forehead against mine. "It's only for two weeks. We'll survive."

Wiggling out of his embrace, I poured myself a cup of coffee, then headed back into the living room, taking a seat on the far end of the sofa. I fixed my gaze on the steam wafting from my cup and hardly spoke to her at all. After Arthur had left for work, I lugged her belongings into the den, yanked open the sofa bed and found her a couple of pillows and sheets. I suggested we both get some sleep.

Without looking at me, she twisted off her copper bracelets, unhooked her sandals, and peeled off her crumpled skirt. "Would it be okay if I put up a wash later?" she asked. "Don't worry, kid, I'll fold my own."

I said of course and shut the door behind me.

I tried to get some sleep but, between Mom and the coffee, I only lay there, my brain surging. Around noon, unable to bear it any longer, I padded back into the den to see how she was doing.

She was sleeping on her side, her mouth open, her damp hair plastered on her forehead from the heat. Above her hung framed blueprints of Arthur's airplanes (I only hoped they weren't inspiring her dreams), and around her stood her cardboard boxes, their flaps gaping, their contents scattered all over the room—a clump of T-shirts on Arthur's desk, a pair of Capri slacks draped over his chair, her sandals tossed by the brass casters of the sofa bed. I sat down on the edge of the mattress and looked at her with dire love, simultaneously experiencing the frightening feeling that once opened and unpacked, these cardboard boxes could never be sealed up again, that even if I got down on my hands and knees and folded and folded and folded, her belongings wouldn't fit back inside them, that I'd never be free of her.

Then, stretching out on the bed beside her, I put my arms around her and dozed off.

Two weeks passed and despite all my efforts, she didn't seem capable of leaving. Sometimes I'd sit up half the night with her, trying to infuse her with her old vim and yearning, only to find her not listening, slouched on the couch, distracted by the drone of the freeway. She *said* she had schemes brewing—something about a memory enhancer vitamin, a breast enlarger night cream—but whenever she'd try out one of her spiels on me, she'd stumble over an unessential point and her eyes would cloud over, their diffuse look of wonder gone.

I didn't want to get Arthur involved but I was at wit's end so I asked him to talk to her, to spell me for a while. It wasn't as if a great change immediately came over her, but after talking to Arthur, she did seem a little more alert, a little less depressed. I couldn't tell if I was hurt by this or relieved. The woman would talk to him for hours, asking him rhetorical questions, rehashing old times, just trying to unpuzzle the enigmatic wanderings of her life. Sometimes Arthur would grow exhausted—my mother was all-consuming—but in his own quiet way, I think he enjoyed their talks, as if by examining her life he was able to see his own from a vantage point I just couldn't provide. While I didn't want to interfere with this, I didn't want her overwhelming him either—and left unchecked, my mother could stagger anyone.

One night, coming downstairs for a glass of water, I overheard her talking to him in the kitchen. It was a quarter past one in the morning. Unable to fathom what she could possibly go on about for hours on end, I crept up to the Dutch doors and put my ear to the crack in the jamb. Speaking in a low, hypnotic murmur, my mother was trying to involve Arthur in one of her mad schemes (an act strictly verboten under my house rules) and Arthur was patiently listening. For a moment I just stood there, trembling on the cold linoleum. Then I yanked open the doors.

"I can't believe you're doing this to me, Mom."

"What?" She glanced over at Arthur and shrugged.

"Involving Arthur in one of your cockamamy scams."

"It's not a scam, Kim, it's a stock tip."

"That's it. You're out!"

"Kim, please," Arthur said.

"It's between my mother and me."

"I don't have a car."

"You can go on foot."

"Kim," Arthur said, "there was no harm being done."

"It's a perfectly legitimate stock," my mother insisted.

"I don't get you, Mom, I really don't. Haven't you made enough of a wreck out of your life without having to make a wreck out of mine?"

She looked incredibly hurt.

"Was that really necessary?" Arthur asked.

"Why the hell are you taking her side?"

"I'm not taking sides. I'm—"

"You know, Kimmy, it might surprise you, but I don't regret the way I've lived my life. Okay, I'm a little sick at heart about losing all my money, and I'm miserable I dumped the trailer, but aside from that, I don't regret—"

"Mom, shut up for a minute! You had no business involving Arthur in another ridiculous, hopeless scam. That was my only rule. One goddamn rule, Mom, and you couldn't follow it!"

"Kim, you don't have to look out for me," Arthur said. "Really, I'm perfectly capable of taking care of myself." He stood up and mashed out his cigarette.

"The woman drove you away in the first place with her mad schemes and her incessant talking and her airplanes and—"

"I left because I was falling in love with you!" And he marched across the linoleum, slamming the Dutch doors behind him.

My mother looked up at me, then down at her coffee cup. I reeled around and headed into the living room, flopping down on the sofa. After a while, she wandered in and joined me.

Neither of us said anything. I had my eyes shut but I knew she was picking at her red ceramic nails—I recognized the familiar scrape, the chalky, brittle digs.

"Kimmy."

"What?"

"Do you really think I'm that much of a loser?"

"Mom, please."

"It's important to me."

"I don't think you're a loser."

"Why did you have to yell at me in front of Arthur?"

"Mom, I—"

"We were just beginning to rebuild our relationship. It's hard enough being here as a third wheel."

"I'm sorry," I said. "It's just that when I heard you trying to involve him in one of your"—she was watching me very closely—"business ventures, I thought . . . I don't know what I thought, Mom. I don't want to lose him."

"Well, I suppose I have driven him a little bonkers in the past."

"Believe me, Mom, you're not the only one."

"If you want me to leave tomorrow, I'll go."

"Forget it."

"It could be a while before things take off for me again."

"I know."

"Do you want me to go upstairs and talk to him, Kimmy?"

"Oh God, Mom, no," I said. "I'll talk to him." Then I leaned over, kissed her leathery cheek, and left her alone in the dark living room, sitting on one end of the sectional sofa.

Arthur was lying on his stomach in bed, his head in his arms. I stretched out beside him on the cold sheets, a foot or two away. Then I let my hand work its way under his cotton T-shirt. I gently stroked him. He didn't say anything. He simply placed his hand over my hand, and pressed it against his chest.

We settled into a routine. My mother would get up first and put up the percolator. If she read the tabloids during breakfast, she didn't discuss them with Arthur and me. Two evenings a week I'd go over her ideas with her, but aside from that, the subject of her business was off limits. Then, one evening in early November, coming home late from work, I opened the backyard gate only to hear her at it again. I headed toward her raspy voice, not sure what I was going to do. The patio stood empty. The night was moonless. Cupping my eye against the rusty screen door, I could just make out the back of Arthur's bowed head, and a couple of feet away, dramatically lit by the dining room chandelier, my mother and her mercurial hands—darting, gesturing, giving to airy nothingness a shape and a weight. The wind kept knocking against the screen, rippling my view and lending to the moment a jittery timelessness, like the jerky motions of old silent films. I couldn't tell if it was the rust or the wind or being left out, but Arthur and my mother looked unbearably old.

I took a step backward, sank down in the hammock, and closed my eyes. For a moment, suspended in the ropes, I experienced the unsettling feeling that the most difficult part of my life hadn't yet begun. And then, just like in one of those old slapstick films, everything went awry. I sat up to let them know I was home and accidentally spilled out of the hammock, crashing to my feet, but because the wind was kicking up, the moon down, they didn't see or hear me. I stood alone on the dark patio, looking in.

That night, lying beside Arthur, I wanted desperately to talk about what I'd seen earlier—not my mother's new attempt at conspiracy but that moment when, through a chance combination of rust and wind and warped screen, I couldn't kid myself any longer.

Instead I said, "You know, we'll probably never be able to get rid of her."

"It was beginning to dawn on me, too, Kim."

"You're not angry?"

He propped himself up on his elbows. "To be frank, I could never quite envision the scenario of us driving her to the edge of the desert and banishing her out there forever."

I forced myself to laugh. Then, sinking a little deeper under the covers, I said, "Arthur, do you ever have a sense of impending danger? I don't know . . . like the three of us are living on top of a hidden fault line, or under the path of a falling meteor?"

He smiled and looked at me curiously.

"Because sometimes I wake up at night, Arthur, thinking that there's something I've forgotten to do to protect us— turn off the gas, lock the door, put up the deflector shields." I turned over and faced the wall. "You don't think I'm going to ruin things for you?"

"Kim," he said, taking me in his arms, "I don't know what you're talking about. Haven't you noticed how happy I've been with you?"

"Come on, Arthur, let's face it. If you stay with me, you're stuck with her. And she'll probably only get worse as she gets older." This was as close as I could come to broaching the subject—the incontestable fact of *his* growing old.

"Kim, try and get some sleep," he said.

I drew up my knees. I crept onto my side of the vast bed and extinguished the light, watching its bright corona fade on the back of my closed lids. For a moment I knew what it was like to be out there alone in cold blue-black space. Then, rolling over, I put my arms around Arthur, so as not to lose my grasp on something solid.

Part Three

The Doppler Effect

Chapter Fifteen

When a train comes toward you, plowing through the immense night, its approach seems interminable; you can hear its whistle and wheels long before you see the silver engine. But once those boxcars clatter past, its wake is minuscule; the train, its cry, the whole noisy caravan vanishes abruptly into a silent wall of darkness. And just that fast, everyone I loved grew old.

We lived together for the next twenty-five years (Arthur and I didn't have the heart to send my mother out there alone again). To please Arthur, for whom the threesome never quite sat right, I legally married him in '73, and to appease my mother, we were wed in a Las Vegas roadside chapel with taped music of her choice (Ravel's "Bolero"). In a snapshot I keep as a memento, you can see the wedding chapel, a pink stucco structure with orange spires, and the bride and groom and the bride's mother to the left of the chapel's pink steps—sun-speared, blanched out, almost unrecognizable against the stark, barren landscape (we are all

listing to one side, dodging handfuls of Minute rice thrown
on us by the two paid witnesses).

The funny thing about watching everyone you love grow
old is that you have to continuously reacquaint yourself with
them. Whenever I come home from a business trip (I sell
scientific equipment on the road now), it takes me at least
a couple of seconds to transmute these elderly strangers into
the people I love. It's not that I've forgotten what they look
like, it's just that . . . you know the sensation . . . You
temporarily forget the perfect word, an important idea, a
loved one's face, and after innumerable seconds of parading
your memory in front of your mind's befuddled eye, you
come across a semblance of the original but it's not exactly
in keeping with your expectations. Of course, after a blink
or two, the elegant gray-haired gentleman turns into my
Arthur again and the sun-wizened old lady . . . well . . .
she transmogrifies into Mom, but there's always that moment of unmitigated sadness when I walk through our front
door and I can't understand why the people I love have left
me behind. And just last week, driving home from a sales
conference, I didn't think I could face it.

I had stopped for a cola at a supermarket. It was early
evening. I was killing time by the magazine racks, waiting
for rush hour to end. All around me I heard the rubber
whoosh of grocery carts, mothers' voices, piped music, the
bells of cash registers. And suddenly I felt that if I couldn't
stop Arthur and my mother from aging, I'd break down here,
in aisle seven, between the copper-topped batteries and the
tabloids. I reached for *The Star* (my mother's favorite paper)
and, just as I did when I was a child, began scouring its
pages for a miracle. What did I have to lose?

And then I saw it, between the ads for baldness cures and the loopy promises of instant beauty, the quintessential story of all our human limitations—Mrs. Robert Fisher, a housewife from Azusa, California, believed she could save her dying husband through the controlled dreams of Astro-Medicine. Did this mean she dreamed of a miracle operation? A genius surgeon in green? A purple-colored pill never tried before? No. Mrs. Robert Fisher, a housewife for over forty years, dreamed that every night her spirit entered her dying husband's veins and got down on its hands and knees and with a small brush and warm solvents scrubbed away the cholesterol deposits along the hundred thousand miles of his failing circulatory system.

I closed the paper and leaned against the cold vending machine. That night, when I got home, I found everyone already asleep—my mother conked out on the sofa, Arthur upstairs in bed. Without waking him, I crawled in beside him and did something I hadn't been able to get myself to do in years. I put my ear on his chest and listened and for one insane moment, inspired by Mrs. Robert Fisher, I tried to envision a safe, durable heart—like the cardboard hearts of chocolate boxes, or the satiny hearts of sofa pillows, or the tiny red hopeful heart my mother had printed on the labels of all her perfume bottles.

"I *feel* lost," my mother said the next morning. I glanced over at Arthur. He was pouring our coffee and he leaned over to kiss me.

"She's been like this ever since you left yesterday," he whispered.

"Really," my mother said aloud, but in a quiet, rapt voice, as if talking to herself, "I keep going over and over my life and I can't figure out what I've accomplished."

She was slouched on the sofa, her frail ankles, with their tributaries of blue veins, raised on the hassock. I perched on the armrest and began massaging her neck, the tiny isthmus between her lunatic head and its aging body.

"Don't be ridiculous," I said. "Remember all your ideas, Mom?"

"That's all they were, Kim, pipe dreams."

"What about the canine treadmills? I believe you sold one or two," Arthur said.

"Oh, I forgot about that."

"Or your Stretch 'n' Tumble exercise classes for the elderly on the beach?"

"Wasn't I going to comb the sand afterward with my metal detector?"

"I believe you did, Mom."

"Perhaps," my mother said, sitting up now, brushing back a wisp of her flyaway hair with her tiny wrist, "perhaps I was just ahead of my time."

"You were always seeing what others didn't."

"And we can't forget my aphrodisiac perfumes."

"We certainly can't," I agreed.

"That was my finest hour. My *la grande vision*. The summit of an entrepreneurial career. I wonder if I hadn't gotten so zealous and insisted on going nationwide, what would have come of it all. Probably just a disaster anyhow."

She picked at her chewed nails, her glass-blue eyes clouding over.

"You know, in some ways, guys, I think I've always longed for disaster. Do you remember drop drills?"

I looked up at Arthur. He shrugged.

"They were after my time, Gloria," he said.

"I never stayed in one school long enough, Mom."

"Well, the teacher would shout 'Drop!' and all us kids were supposed to fall to our knees at her feet. You know I don't care for authority, guys, but I would fall like the rest and take on the pose of a supplicant. And I remember one day ducking under my desk and hoping not for an atom bomb explosion with its abrupt vaporization but for a soft rolling earthquake and the possibility that the schoolhouse, my house, the whole neighborhood, would crash all around me, like a house of cards, and through the rubble, I would hear a voice, the voice of someone I deemed important as a child— say, a fireman or a police chief—calling and calling to *me* alone, 'Where are you, Gloria, where are you?' "

I was becoming increasingly worried about her. She didn't seem to be wholly of this world anymore. Sometimes the three of us would be talking together at the kitchen table and poof—she'd fall asleep, her elbows on the Formica, her coffee getting cold. She'd look so old and vanquished and frail that I'd immediately try to get her to lie down, but Arthur would stop me. "It's not necessary," he'd assure me, continuing to eat his corn flakes, "she's comfortable. She just wants to be near you when you're not traveling, Kim." I'd try to finish my breakfast without constantly looking over at her, snoring raggedly, chin slack against chest, tiny shoulders hunched. And then, just as unexpectedly, she'd snap out of it and resume whatever she was saying in midsentence, and Arthur would answer her.

Or I'd come home from a business trip late at night only

to find she'd fallen asleep on Arthur's La-Z-Boy, listening
to her *How to Succeed at Business and Retire at the Same Time*
records. One rainy evening, the front door was left wide
open, the needle was skipping, her headphones sat askew,
pressing against her temples like two electric shock pads.

I fetched her a blanket and gently removed them.

"Most of you . . . most of you . . . most of you," a
faint mechanical voice intoned, "haven't made time . . .
time . . . time . . . to live the life for which you were
destined. This is what ages you . . . ages you . . . ages
you . . . this and nothing more."

Or, with her eyes failing, unable to read the tabloids at
night, she'd sit up till ungodly hours, watching television,
drifting in and out of sleep, her dreams influenced by the
news specials and docudramas on sex, mercenaries, loneliness, disease, war, and natural disasters, until every global
squabble and calamity would appear before her as a person-
alized message. If a volcano blew up on Java or a gas main
exploded in downtown LA, she dreamed she was standing
on the lip of each and every crater.

One night she roused Arthur and me from sleep because
she swore she saw our old house, the one we'd lived in after
the accident, collapsing in a mud slide on one of the news
programs: okay, the landscaping looked different, the whole
roof had been sliced off by a wall of dirt, but she was sure
it was ours.

And my patient, tolerant Arthur wrapped himself in his
Scotch plaid robe and followed her into the den.

I lingered for a while in bed. "Arthur," I called, "what
the hell is she talking about?"

"It's difficult to say."

I heard rain outside and on the TV (in her old age, my

mother listened with the volume at deafening decibels). And I heard a crack that must have come from within the television set but sounded like a seam opening in the crust of the earth.

"Kim, I can't believe it but I think your mother is right."

I hurried into the den.

Rain slanted across the television screen. A tiny raincoated figure stood next to a reporter and waved at the camera.

"Earlier today Mrs. Buck's home, and all her possessions, washed away," the reporter reported.

In an insert on the bottom of the screen, we watched Mrs. Buck's sofa—a cherry-red antique with matching armchairs—disappear under a deluge of mud.

"That's just the kind of furniture I should have bought when I had money," my mother said.

"This must come as a horrible shock to you, Mrs. Buck," the reporter said.

The tiny raincoated figure shrugged.

"The folks out there are really rooting for you and your family. Is there anything you'd like to tell them?"

"I'd just like to say that at such and such an address, Mrs. Buck once lived. Nothing more. Just that."

"Thank you, Mrs. Buck," the reporter said.

"May I say something else?" the woman asked.

"Of course."

"Doesn't the governor fly over disasters in an airplane?"

The reporter looked puzzled.

"Perhaps," I joked, glancing over at my mother, "perhaps Mrs. Buck is referring to your phantom jumbo jet, Mom," but my mother had fallen asleep, and Arthur was nodding off too.

"Do you mean a helicopter, Mrs. Buck?" the reporter corrected her.

"Whatever. Will you be flying with him?"

"I don't know."

"Well, if you do fly with him, or if you fly above here with anyone else who is famous, will you be sure to mention me by name. Just say that at such and such an address, Mrs. Buck once lived."

I started to get up to turn off the television but the instant I budged, Arthur and my mother murmured in their sleep. So I just sat there, stock-still, on the sofa beside them.

My right foot went to sleep. Then my leg. Then I too must have drifted off because when I looked up again, my mother was leaning forward, elbows on knees, eyes unblinking, staring intently at the flickering image—a tiny figure wandering over a muddy landscape, amid eerie wreckage—and for a moment, slightly discombobulated, I thought Mrs. Buck was still on. But nothing looked familiar. It turned out to be a docudrama on the discovery of Pompeii.

I couldn't imagine why my mother was so interested. I peeked over Arthur's sleeping profile, scrunched on the cushions between us, and watched her as she scrutinized archaeologist Giuseppe Fiorelli trudging over a clueless landscape swinging a mechanical dowsing wand, not unlike her metal detector. He kept stumbling upon uncharted holes, tapping into them. But all he found was the rank air of time, leaving him with a mysterious absence of something. He filled these chasms with plaster. He exhumed the dry casts, each one solidifying into a human form where it had fallen—a woman clutching a billowy space as if weeping into a pillow, a man with a smudge of ashen fluff, like a crumb, hanging from his open lips. Once cleaned, my mother took note, these pieces were auctioned to museums. But Giuseppe knew, and I know, that what man had left in the sealed chambers of Pompeii was the indelible shape of his emotions.